Shackles of Conformity

Book 2: Psychological Freedom

Mark Hammond Baker

Copyright © 2022 Mark Hammond Baker

All rights reserved

The characters and events portrayed in this book are fictitious. Any similarity to real persons, living or dead, is coincidental and not intended by the author.

No part of this book may be reproduced, or stored in a retrieval system, or transmitted in any form or by any means, electronic, mechanical, photocopying, recording, or otherwise, without express written permission of the publisher.

ISBN-13: 9798410867290
ISBN-10: 1477123456

Cover design by: Art Painter
Library of Congress Control Number: 2018675309
Printed in the United States of America

CONTENTS

Title Page
Copyright
Psychological Freedom   5
Chapter 1   7
Chapter 2   16
Chapter 3   23
Chapter 4   28
Chapter 5   32
Chapter 6   34
Chapter 7   42
Chapter 8   48
Chapter 9   52
Chapter 10   60
Chapter 11   66
Chapter 12   73
Chapter 13   84
Chapter 14   96
Chapter 15   107
Chapter 16   111
Chapter 17   120

Chapter 18	127
Chapter 19	143
Chapter 20	150
Chapter 21	154
Chapter 22	157
Chapter 23	161
Chapter 24	167
Chapter 25	174

This book is dedicated to my grandmother, Miriam Lynn May. She has been fighting cancer for the past six years and plans on being successful with her chemo-therapy treatments and continuing to live out the rest of her life. I would also like to send out immense positive vibes to my best friend Treva Gregg. Other people who cannot be left out because of their help and support include my friends: Mini Hawthorn, Sean Sartin, Alex Burchnell, Cynthia Comans, Maurice Collins, Renee Allen, Ashton Johnson, Randy Julian, Cynthia Loper, Colt Allen, and Christopher Noto. Finally, a special thanks to Dr. Allen Johnson from Encounter Community Counseling for helping me overcome some of life's difficulties.

Carpe diem is a value system I hold in high esteem. In life, I would like to emulate this philosophical perspective. As a leader, I count on people who have gone through difficult times and who've encountered the type of problems that songs in today's music (as well as stories from the Bible) have illustrated, to better understand that life is good. The story of our struggles is far more profound and impacting than having a picture-perfect life. Accepting my salvation through faith in Christ Jesus has aided in my ability to live a life full of joy. My conviction that God's grace through Jesus is more powerful than any evil that may come my way is experienced spiritually through the following verse, "I can do all things through Christ who strengthens me." (Philippians 4:13) This isn't the easiest life in the world, but it is still a good life. We're all just doing the best we can, and we have to let go of all that extra stuff holding us back. Seize the day! Embrace it and live it up to the fullest, but we must also be wise, but not so wise that we miss out on all the fun; the important thing is to have fun.

Psychological Freedom

Written by Mark Hammond Baker

Disclaimer: Any likeness or resemblance of characters to real individuals is strictly coincidence. Author does not encourage abuse of substances or breaking the law to partake in such behavior. Use discretion and be responsible.

MARK HAMMOND BAKER

I would like to express how helpful my Editor-in-Chief, Christopher Burchnell, was while writing this book. If you ever have the chance to get to know the guy, I'd recommend it. His helpful insight made it easy to throw ideas around for designing the plot of this novel. Having a keen ability to discuss societal issues which inspired this second book brought me face to face with someone who was real and has shown love to me like a brother through Christ. One remarkable personality trait about Mr. Chris is his incredible courage; courage that is unparalleled and stressed by his reserved nature. Being connected with him and his husband through constructive social media relationships made this work possible. Thank you!

PSYCHOLOGICAL FREEDOM

Written by Mark H. Baker,

Edited by Chris Burchnell

Preface

This narrative takes off from where my last entry ended. I have done my best to describe the most important events and provide an answer to every question. The purpose of this was so that readers, especially Alward, would be able to form a clear picture of what took place. In doing so, perhaps a lesson on kindness can be drawn. If there is a moral to this story it is that pursuing peace is a task that will always lay ahead, as the journey to create healthy relationships and build bridges is never over. This book largely depicts the psychological nature of leadership and also presents a philosophical dilemma to the reader. That dilemma is primarily about how much trust and authority administrative decision makers should have.

Reading about the events in this story will hopefully leave an impression that will cause us to question humanity's place in the universe. What will happen when other forms of life are discovered, and are we prepared to handle it? This novel brings up the topics like criminal justice, morality, and hope. The main idea here prompts us to ask, is humanity ready to engage with other societies of intelligent beings who may be alive in this galaxy? Would taking away free will be a solution to the problem of breaking the peace, or is this simply a problem that we should indefinitely anticipate?

CHAPTER 1

Before delving in to the remainder of the story, let's recap the episodes leading up to our current situation. Supreme Commander Malcolm was second in command to Lord Komodo. She handled oversight on Planet Earth pertaining to carrying out political correctness and was likewise the authority who sanctioned social protocols. She spent most of her time in her spaceship orbiting the Earth as she did not want to be infected with the virus which would cause people to later be called mind slaves. Keep in mind though that during the time this part of history was taking place, there were also two dozen other planets enslaved by Lord Komodo, each of which had a person with the equivalent of Malcolm's title maintaining order.

The power Lord Komodo had gained politically was through the use of his strategic intelligence, which was shown time and time again to be on a genius level. He claimed himself to be a servant of peace, but many people considered him to be dangerous. This was mainly because he expected and was granted absolute reverence by the Council of Planets within the Orion Arm of the Milky Way. This respect was brought about primarily because of his methods for handling criminals- criminals of which he was appointed to "rehabilitate" by the council.

Komodo's job caused him to be hailed as a dictator, but this was only somewhat accurate. This, along with his political influence, caused the people in the free world suspicious of him. So far, two dozen out of one hundred and fifty-two planets known to have sentient life in the Orion Arm of the Milky-Way Galaxy had fallen under the domination of Komodo. The Millennial virus, which was identified as the 2084 pathogen, was at first only wielded against criminals, but it was subsequently employed to take away the free will of entire planetary civilizations. With the eradication of free will came the elimination of any risk posed against the peace; planets prone to go to war or who had a significant crime rate were issued the virus. Yet, for this to be allowed by the Orion Arm Council of Planets in the first place, the legislative body had to get a minimum of a three-fourths vote.

At the poll, out of the 152 votes possible (one tally for each world but there were far more council members than that), 113 members voted yes while 37 voted nays. Finally, the tie breaker was to be determined by a person native to my friend Orthopox's world, who was also a Pastafarian, to produce the final determination. The Nibiruīian psychological organism, whose name was Slemrod, was placed on the spot so much so that he at first renounced his membership with the Orion Arm Council of Planets.

Komodo, knowing Slemrod was in police security and that any interference on his behalf would delegitimize the vote, did the next best thing. He recommended that if the Millennial 2084 mind control could not be used, then the council must plan for war by using one of his planets, or multiple, to establish armies in the name of all that is peaceful.

The volume of pressure continued to expand on Slemrod as more and more was placed on the line. Without an hour to afford, when it looked like Komodo would start producing weapons of mass destruction, it was up to Slemrod to decide the fate of the vote. Komodo was not hesitant to make outlandish threats to ensure his interventions were made as efficiently as possible, as his primary mission was to take care of the people on his home world, and to him that meant applying the 2084 virus to any threat. Slemrod cast his ballot, which immediately granted the Space Rangers permission to put their plan into action; this meant infecting planets who posed a threat to the peace with the Millennial 2084 virus.

The moral leadership of Komodo's home world of Reperoritas condemned his ascent up the political ladder. Mainly this is because they were aware of his distorted way of setting up statues of himself on the enslaved worlds and requiring the mindless rule-followers to revere him as Lord Komodo. Since the sacred leaders on Reperoritas would never tolerate this to happen on their planet, they undermined his profession and censured him from their social graces.

What couldn't be denied was that Komodo provided more profit for his species than they had ever seen prior to the establishment of The System of Correction, which was done by terraforming the other planets in his solar system and allowing the council to use them to rehabilitate criminals. Sadly, the leadership of Reperoritas did not see things from his point of view, despite their newfound wealth, which forced Komodo to work alone all while enduring a lot of criticism.

Well, after Jamie Southerns and King Thaddeus escaped from Malcolm's spaceship, the supreme commander gave scant regard to the Polunin king. Being only somewhat conscious of the audacious spirit of the underwater monarch, she lapsed to recognize he planned on using everything he had learned while he was held captive to put a stop to the radical social injustice taking place on his planet.

If you remember, the great King Thaddeus lived an aquatic life and, as a member of The Orion Arm Council of Planets, he wore a suit that allowed him to walk on land. It came to great surprise when they asked him to sign a form granting approval for underwater fisherman to trap a certain percentage of the population of his people each year. They could later alter the Pelages that were caught into drugs. Yet, Thaddeus refused the council's offer to be economically compensated by passionately referring to the council's constitution, which declared that killing sentient life was an infraction against the peace.

It was thus that a coalition formed who felt the drug manufactured from the body parts of the people of Polunin was indispensable medication. Their political alliance grew until they convinced Supreme Commander Malcolm to abduct the King Thaddeus, which she did and placed on the shelf in her office aboard the mothership orbiting Earth. Of course, when Thaddeus was large enough to sum up to human stature when wearing his above water. Though, by himself he was only about two feet high excluding his very large tentacles. The same vessel that took around one hundred thousand Space Rangers, the name given to them because it was the job the council assigned to them, to Earth when they first invaded.

After that, the people of Polunin publicly accused the morally corrupt leaders, who allowed illegal fishing of sentient life to take place on their planet. A trial followed in which the Orion Judicial Council had no option but to trust the word of Thaddeus' twin, Gregory. The corrupt individual who became the new king after Thaddeus had surreptitiously been taken away, predominantly because Gregory gave the drug cartel information to be used to do so.

Of course, after Jamie Southerns and Thaddeus had escaped, Malcolm's awareness of his existence never roamed far from her mind. This was because he once stood as a living trophy within a large jar on her shelf in the commander's room. Though, in her mind the king had been conquered and once he was dead his species would be extinct. This was something she wasn't proud of, but she herself was a consumer of Jellyfish Juice.

Before the Space Rangers had learned of his planet and the ability of King Thaddeus's people, the Pelages, to provide a sort of high by literally consuming their flesh, kind King Thaddeus had reigned over the planet Pelages benevolently. Through civil wars and the climate crisis, King Thaddeus, a marine creature resembling a jellyfish with amazing feats of strength, agility, and intelligence, had seen his people through all hardships. Later in this story's timeline, they would give him the title of the greatest king who ever lived.

The Pelages people, through incomparable feats of architecture unknown to any other species, had constructed an underwater metropolis. They set up this breathtaking underwater city with a strong economy that was all but utopian and alive with a people whose spirits were furnished with untold tranquility.

Well, the story goes as I, Arnold Fitzgerald, write this from remembrance, that after getting wind of our main characters having been taken away from the mission at hand, Thaddeus began searching for a means to continue liberating all the planets the Space Rangers had enslaved. Primarily, he needed to deliver the antidote-vaccine combination to all the people who had been affected. This was because Thaddeus and the minority of council members from the Council of Planets (those who voted against the implementation of the pathogen to use on criminals) wanted to put an end to the tyranny of the Space Rangers.

To do this, he reflected on the species who had been most instrumental in supporting this war on personal liberty in the past- the Ancient Ones. The Ancients were the first life-forms ever known to have existed in the Milky Way. There were many rumors of how The Ancient Ones came to live in the Milky Way- one being that they used their advanced technology to transport themselves here from another galaxy.

Supposedly, they moved here so that they could run some experiments in a galaxy void of life. Experiments that comprised harvesting entire stars to fuel their spaceships. The theory was that over time they would habitat on different planets and while they were there, they would release different animals that would later emerge as sentient life. Put it this way, The

Ancients are a species who have been around for over a billion years; many of them lived many millions of years but never seemed to grow old. If you are interested in knowing why I am mentioning them now, keep reading.

Thaddeus had discovered the coordinates to The Ancient's planet via a star chart that he and Jamie had worked together to steal from the Space Rangers. How Lord Komodo found it was by doing what was in his first nature, by being an archeologist. I'm not sure what planet in this sector he discovered the star map on, but when he did, he wasn't even sure what it was. But he believed it was the artifactual remains of a species that had once inhabited the planet and had long since left.

It just so happened that while Thaddeus and Jamie were fleeing from Malcolm's ship that Thaddeus took it with him. After all that time sitting on the shelf watching people from his planet get eaten, he had wondered about this map Malcolm studied diligently. At the last instant while escaping, Thaddeus telepathically instructed Jamie, who had been under the influence of Millennium 27-864 (people later began calling it the 2084 virus), to take the map because he wanted his lead scientist to have a look at it; God willing they survive escape.

So, although Jamie had been thoroughly deprived of her ability to act of her own volition because of the pathogen, Thaddeus constructed a cognitive relationship with her. Both of them escaped Malcolm's ship with the star chart and found what they knew could only be temporary refuge within the still undiscovered Prism City on Thaddeus' home planet of Polunin.

After that, as the story goes, while in Prism City and still under the influence of Millennium 27-864, Jamie Southerns worked with Polunin's lead scientist, Dr. Ramos Destin Uphanivan to decode the map which included a formula that could send a signal all the way to the Pegasus Arm of the Milky Way. The scientist was successful at sending the signal primarily due to how he skilled he was at interpreting the directions on the star map, which acted sort of like a key.

While Jamie and Thaddeus were waiting on a response from the Pegasus Arm, they organized for the 37 council members who voted nay to meet with them on Polunin. While contacting the council members, Jamie, still under the influence of the pathogen, discovered that Sid was in trouble via his distress beacon. Her personal spaceship, which she had sequestered from the Space Rangers, made it just in time to save us. By the time Jamie, Sid, Samuel, Orthopox and I returned to Polunin (upon invitation from King Thaddeus), Ramos Destin Uphanivan had received a response from The Ancients, which included a date and location to meet with them.

To make a long story short, The Ancient Ones admitted to being responsible for initially developing the mind controlling virus; in fact, they ran into the same problem we did. The virus was not safe; according to The Ancients, it caused organisms to de-evolve, and this was a breach of contract.

After millions of years, a rather rambunctious Ancient had developed an antidote and liberated everyone who had been infected in the galaxy; it was only later that a planet left unvaccinated was discovered, which was how the virus came to be used once again. She came to be known as The Rebel and secretly created intelligent colonies all over the Milky Way in hopes of one day using us to overthrow the autocracy the Ancient Ones' civilization had become. I came to know about all of this through the telepathic communication that took place the first time we had contact with the Ancient Ones during our first contact with them that took place during a council meeting.

On Planet Svetlana, the council meeting with The Ancients ended, and we landed this spaceship in the parking area nearer Sid's apartment and took a flying taxi cab the rest of the way. We all thought it seemed promising now that a cure to the virus was in hand, but after flying up to the apartment doors via a taxi, all hell broke loose.

Malcolm was sitting in the apartment just waiting for us to get there, and that's when Samuel Yellowstone, my boyfriend, attempted to kill her. The bad news is that he was too slow and he was shot instead, dying instantly. I have never been so heartbroken as I was on that day. Samuel Yellowstone was my first love. I still remember his dark brown eyes looking directly into mine and knowing that this person was my friend who I loved and cared deeply about. It wasn't until much later that we became boyfriends, and we only did so because our bond outgrew friendship and overflowed into a passionate love for each other.

Just as the war on personal liberty was about to be victorious, Sid, Orthopox, Samuel, and myself were captured by Malcolm. This happened before the Council of Planets had determined the best course of action to take in liberating the dozens of worlds that had been seized by the clutches of the Space Rangers. It is here where our story continues.

Keenly aware of The Rebel's plan to usurp the oppressors, and in doing so make a stance against conformity and intellectual slavery, King Thaddeus began scheming of the best way to contact her after Malcolm had captured me, along with Sid and Orthopox. The rest of The Ancient Ones, though appearing as if they were indifferent, were still interested to see if humanity were capable of existing in the Galactic Council.

x

Malcolm had discovered the four of us while waiting for us to enter Sid's apartment. The Supreme Commander then ordered for Sid to be arrested and interrogated for any information regarding The Ancients and our plans. This was because as captain, she suspected he knew the most. But before that happened, my boyfriend at the time took hold of a pistol Sid had in his back pocket and pointed it at the face of social conformity, the supreme commander. Then his finger hesitated a moment too long on the trigger, giving the guards enough time to gun him down. His bullet wounds killed him instantly, and his body fell limp into my arms.

Once Samuel's lifeless body was pried out of my arms, Malcolm ordered that Orthopox and I to be sent to The System of Correction. The planet of that solar system, which was the same system that the Space Ranger's home planet Reperoritas was in, that had become the place to send people who either the free will inhibiting virus did not affect or who had received preventative immunization properties against it, was called Zumumbufum.

We were sentenced to work at the main headquarters of the mining facility on Zumumbufum, which maintained all the rigs all over the planet. The rigs pumped Xubuntos from out beneath the ground. Both decisions that Malcolm made concerning me and my team were to satisfy the politically correct agenda that the Council of Planets had approved the Space Rangers to carry out. All of their motives were supposedly based on establishing and maintaining peace in the Orion Arm of the Milky Way, at least between the planets that technology made it possible to visit.

CHAPTER 2

Here is where the rest of the story begins. The mining facility on Zumumbufum had been organized monotonously. Every prisoner had a uniform that displayed their company number. Orthopox and I could hardly speak to each other except during mealtimes, but our supervisor was never far enough away to where we could plan and discuss an escape plan. The guards were not concerned about any of us escaping, though. This was because apart from the facility, the rest of the world was uninhabitable.

At one point, Zumumbufum had been abundant with life but had since become a desert wasteland. The mining facility started out as a struggle to stabilize the atmosphere so that the planet could be terraformed, but because of the financial situation, it soon became obvious that mining Xubuntos was more profitable. Of course, at first, they did not know that Xubuntos was indeed present on the planet, and that is why the Resienian Empire had no issue selling the planet to the Space Rangers.

Eventually, a lawsuit resulted that the Resienian ended up losing. It was over the Space Rangers not being upfront with their knowledge that the fuel source was present on Zumumbufum; but the Orion Judicial Council still ruled in favor of the Space Rangers because that was not required. Finally, the terraforming facility was remodeled into a much larger mining facility that was run by the Space Rangers, who used convicts as the people who did the hard labor; they did so in order to get less of a prison sentence.

The Zumumbufum facility looked as boring and uniform

as the rest of the construction projects the Space Rangers had completed. The main headquarters was the size of a small city, while mining rigs all over the planet often spurted large spouts of fire and smoke. When the prisoners doing forced labor went back to their chambers at headquarters they were covered in sticky black oil. Well, I had been given a job as a telecommunications operator whereby I directed calls and relayed messages to the proper departments; with the use of his translator, Orthopox also was employed with a similar job.

There were no art pieces in the facility and very scant sources of entertainment, aside from what happened during the educational programing designed to create new neural pathways of learning, which was essentially obedience training. Yet, there were televisions all over the campus that broadcasted the daily updates about the new administration from the newsroom on the third floor. Also, news about people who completed their sentence on Zumumbufum was broadcasted over the televisions. Former prisoners did not usually break away from the new societal norms as doing so would mean immediate relocation to the System of Correction (aka the prison planet of Zumumbufum within the Space Ranger solar system).

The main building was three stories high (in the middle of the desert that a person could only survive in for twenty-four hours or fewer without a spacesuit depending on species) with smaller buildings wrapping around into a loop. As for personal quarters, each person was assigned a room by themselves, and the housing area had the capacity of around fifteen hundred individuals, though we did not use that term as it was the opposite of what we felt like it here. It wasn't so much a home as a prison.

Large crafts like what you would see in the Gulf Coast pumped the Xubuntos from underneath the wasteland. Fuel that was used to power spaceships which sold at steep prices. This substance was the remains of thousands of years of radioactive materials that had been left there from planets all over the

Orion Arm. Special precautions were taken so that the workers did not gain genetic mutations while obtaining it. Finally, having broken down enough to be used as fuel, the Space Rangers correctly followed the Orion Arm Council of Planets' directions and went by all the proper procedures; yet occasionally someone would die from radiation poisoning and afterwards all evidence of that person simply disappeared from the computer system. We were said to be criminals after all- who cared if a few of us never existed.

While still in our right minds, Orthopox and I had a memorial service for Samuel Yellowstone, my fallen hero of a boyfriend. Of course, we did not have a body, and the only thing belonging to him I still had in my possession at the time was a shirt of mine that had his blood on it from when Malcolm's guards shot and killed him. With the proper paperwork and reluctant approval by Malcolm, we were allowed with guards to venture out of the facility, where we found a large boulder to use as a memorial site. We said prayers for Sam, whom we knew was fully affirmed by Jesus.

I shed many tears and clung onto Orthopox's thick pink fur for many minutes. What was going to happen to my species? I told myself I had to do what Sam would want me to do, which was to continue fighting for humanity's freedom. Although we were totally defeated, I knew that King Thaddeus, Jamie, Sid, and other members of the Council of Planets were out there.

It wasn't clear what they were currently doing or how much progress the treachery of the Space Rangers had made, but what was certain was that there was a flame of righteousness inside me that would not be quenched, that would not be blown out, cast down, or extinguished… if there was ever something I could do, I would be there and I would do it. My voice would never be silenced now that I had been vaccinated against the virus. I would do everything in my power, what little of it I may have, to contribute to the usurping of Malcolm and her regime. I was going to find a way off of Zumumbufum; never would I lift a finger for scum like Malcolm... or so I thought.

x

What could we do? This was a question I shared with Orthopox as we made our way back to the facility because there was no way to survive anywhere else on the planet. The reason they had sent Orthopox and me to Zumumbufum was to mine Xubuntos while receiving educational programming, which helped us comply with Malcolm's system. Of course, Malcolm was a servant of Lord Komodo, who had power over many planets. Power seized by using the virus to take control.

My first idea was to start an uprising amongst the inmates. Now, I was never a violent man, but this monster had taken the love of my life away from me. So, the way I saw it, killing a few of her guards, or at least immobilizing them if possible, and even her in the process wasn't simply an act of revenge... it was justice.

When we got back to the facility, we were once again separated from each other. Since nothing personal could be exchanged between staff members nor between prisoners and staff, which primarily comprised Space Rangers, we both let out a sigh of defeat. Orthopox had his pink fur cut down to his bare skin and likewise, for my hair to take away a sense of identity. My individuality was once again stricken as I was assigned the label: Prisoner 40586. Both Orthopox and I were both forced to wear gray prison gowns- Orthopox especially, since his exotic reproductive system that was not fully understood by the Rangers, and was fully exposed without his fur.

Upon first arriving at Zumumbufum, I observed that the Space Rangers were enslaved by their own social protocol themselves. Yet, they seemed to worship this protocol, something they gloated and boasted about; as was evidenced by the re-educational processes and daily rituals they instilled in the prisoners.

Each day seemed to blur together and did not differ from the next. Although we had been given the serum by The Ancients- a race of aliens whose intelligence could not be measured via the intelligence quotient given by psychologists on Earth because their knowledge and intellect surpassed anything known to humankind- which cured and prevented the extinction of a person's ability to act on their own free will because of Millennial 2084, it didn't matter. In less than a month, Malcolm had solved that issue.

Once she observed how some prisoners who had taken the vaccine refused to do the work her operation demanded, she designed a new treatment of oral medication that would override the vaccination thus causing a dramatic decline in cognitive awareness and the ability to behave freely. The new serum was called Soma and was given to people and life-forms who had been vaccinated against the free will immobilizing virus. I had to be seen by a doctor, per the official protocol of the Council of Planets, in order for the medication to be legally prescribed; this wasn't very fair, but as a prisoner I had lost my right to appeal. But before I began the medication regimen, I met a few people who had taken the vaccine.

In fact, I witnessed the intellectual transformation that took place once it was given many times. Even on Zumumbufum, there grew a group of liberated intellectuals who felt a radical injustice was taking place. The intellectual elite on Zumumbufum felt they would rather risk their lives trying to escape and plead their case to leadership that they hoped were righteous.

One such person went by the name of Rufus Deertail. He was a tall handsome male humanoid figure who I found out was from the planet Decorus, which was about a dozen stars north of the Earth's Sun. Rufus called himself Decorian, but in reality, nobody was actually born on Decorus because it was a planet that was home to only homosexuals.

Apparently, the Space Rangers had gotten wind of this type of behavior and used Millennium 27-864 to enslave the entire planet, thereafter re-educating them to be heterosexual. Yet Rufus had stowed away on a cargo ship, where he had to survive on space rats for weeks. While being a stowaway, he had met someone with a temporary antidote. When he was finally discovered by the Space Rangers, he took the temporary antidote right before they gave him the Millennium 27-864. He remained an intellectual until he was discovered and brought to Zumumbufum for his insubordination. The details about his life's story will be accounted for later on.

Without the virus Millennium 27-864, the Space Rangers felt that they would have made no progress in solving the problem of war and crime. There were hundreds of criminals from peaceful planets who were purposely infected that had to be reintegrated into society so that they would do whatever they were told. Also, Komodo felt that if he was successful in solving the problem of crime, finding The Ancient Ones would be even easier but so far, he had no luck in solving the star map or cracking the formula written on it.

Even though the original had been stolen, he had made plenty of copies of it. Yet, he had heard from his sources that The Ancients had been in contact with the body of council members who opposed him using the virus on criminals, which was why they remained in hiding.

It was said that The Ancient Ones have technology that can increase intelligence and spacecraft that can jump from one galaxy to the next nearly instantaneously; how the Space Rangers imagined they would defeat a race of beings like this was beyond my comprehension. To Komodo, this technology seemed a more viable option to establish peace, though many millions of people thought he was evil. Truth be told, Komodo was a perfectionist who only wanted to see his people out of poverty; still, he was hated and despised for what he was doing.

Although Orthopox and I had been separated shortly after arriving at the mining facility, just after the funeral for Samuel, I was sure that if I was being given the medication, so was he. Each time we took it, not only had we become the physical prisoners of the Space Rangers, but they could now control our minds. We were psychological slaves.

The first dose was agonizing, not physically, but mentally. I had never had my free will stripped away from me, but as the medication crept through my veins, I felt my ability to think for myself slowly dissipating. I took the last few minutes. I had to move around freely of my volition as well as to make a few autonomous comments about how one day there would be an intellectual liberation. While doing so, I witnessed the guards wait in anticipation for the medication to kick in so that they could begin giving me orders.

After the first hour of taking the medication, I began doing whatever I was told and questioned nothing. Each morning before mealtime, they would administer my medication to me. After a few days, the guards no longer needed to administer the medication to me personally because I had been instructed to administer it to myself. Inwardly, I knew that because I was on this medication, I was expected to act a certain way. I was not free to speak my mind, but waited to be told what to think. I did my best to allow the re-educational programming to strike me of any kind of uniqueness that would cause me to alert the attention of the social protocol police.

CHAPTER 3

They had given us specific jobs at the mining facility; at the time I was not sure what Orthopox was doing, nor did I even think of him. In fact, I had no thoughts of my own besides what had been taught to me through the re-education process that took place daily. My job was in telecommunications. Basically, I was an operator and gave daily announcements over the intercom. I never saw or thought of Orthopox until I began hearing voices.

I reported my symptoms to the guards as they taught me to do, but they only laughed at me. The voices would tell me that my pills were being replaced with placebos and that I should expect achieving a state of psychological emancipation, and this scared me because I knew thinking independently was a violation in procedure. I did not want to believe the voices, but I would hear them while walking in the corridors and especially while lying awake at night.

The voices started telling me things that made little sense such as things like my assumptions are wrong. That the medication wasn't working. The voices would tell me I was too smart to waste my mind. It was all very confusing, and since the voices were coming from out of nowhere I thought I had gone crazy. And the voices laughed at me when I cried in defeat. In an episode of agony, I begged the voices to stop, to leave me alone. That is when riddles started.

"Arnold, we will stop if you can answer us one riddle!" said an ominous voice.

I hesitated because I was not sure where these voices were coming from or why they would want me to answer a riddle. I left my work station and found a quiet place to sit in one of the bathroom stalls. The munchkin-like voice then continued with his riddle:

"I am a type of speech that causes people confusion.

I am neither helpful nor am I coherent.

Some say I am meaningless.

I do not work in a straightforward manner.

Guess what I am?"

I sat there for several seconds with my mind clouded in thought as I attempted to understand free thinking, but no answer came. After a few more minutes went by, a menagerie of voices laughed at me.

"And the answer is, RIGMAROLE! You see Arnold, you need our help. Would you like to try again or admit that you need us more than we need you?" said the voice whose woodland accent was becoming more apparent.

"Very well!" I stammered. "I'll try again." Then the voice continued relaying his riddle.

"It is a bad communication habit.

Done instead of having ideas.

Guards like it since it wastes time.

Doing this accomplishes nothing."

Again, I sat on the toilet trying my best to think of an answer but more anxious about being away from my workstation.

"Ah-ha! We've defeated you yet again. The answer to this riddle is, to squabble!" said the unknown voice who was making me think I really had lost my mind.

"The last riddle I will leave you to answer for yourself," said the voice. "What is as obvious as the paint on this wall but as difficult to realize as a stubborn ox?"

I knew the answer to that one right away. It was that I needed their help.

I stormed out of the bathroom and altered the guards who reported this to Malcolm. In response, Malcolm ordered the doctor to increase the dosage of my medication and reintroduced the idea of taking them in front of the guards. They still could not explain why I was having thoughts that had nothing to do with my job, why I was speaking out of turn, or how it was possible for me to go above and beyond in my duties to please my superiors. My feelings and re-education were not matching up, and this terrified me in my vulnerable state.

Still, every morning, I and the other prisoners would be given our medication and told to resume our everyday duties. I knew I was sick because I felt like going back to sleep instead of obeying the chain of command and fulfilling my daily duties like I had been told. Eventually, I listened to the voices.

"Do what they say, don't give them any sign that you hear us or they will put you back in solitary confinement," said an ominous voice to me on the morning of our weekly worship of Lord Komodo. I did what the voices said because I was afraid of what might happen to me if I didn't.

"If you tell them you can hear us, nobody will believe you," I would hear through the vents in my room.

"Once they know you aren't compliant, they will kill you," said the voice another time.

During what had to have been a year into being at the work camp and months after the voices started communicating with me, I snapped during our worship service for Lord Komodo. In tears, I fell to my knees and began appealing to Christ instead of Komodo.

"Jesus, I need you now more than ever before. I feel out of control and I cannot endure living with being forced to make my own decisions. Please make these voices go away!" I begged as I snagged a laser gun from the guards and positioned it towards my head. This was when the guards knew something was dreadfully awry and committed me to the hospital.

Malcolm again increased the dosage of my medication; this time the Soma worked, and I was back in perfect bliss as I had not one thought of my own and was thoroughly comfortable following rules and not reasoning about why.

"They gave him another dosage of Soma and we didn't replace it in time!" I heard voices speaking to each other. When I reported this to the proper authorities, they understood me as suffering from schizophrenia. Instead of returning to my normal duties, I was brought to the psychiatric hospital where I was held as a patient. At that point, I was both a detainee and a patient, but I was advised not to even think about those types of things by my doctor.

Re-education proceeded in a much more vigorous way than ever before. The voices told me they were still replacing my medicine with a placebo, but the Chamaeleonidae nurse didn't even record that because she had been told I was suffering from delusions- probably as a side effect of too much Xubuntos in the air. I must have been severely allergic.

I stopped reporting what the voices were saying when the doctors began administering heavy sedatives to me, mainly because I was too doped up to pay attention. The guards didn't believe me anyway, even if I told them the voices were organizing a way for me to escape. All they did was cuff my arm to the bedside.

x

I was informed that my condition was growing increasingly worse when I reported mice were clambering around my hospital room at night.

"Arnold, these are only hallucinations. We are going to keep you here until we have your condition under control. Although you are our prisoner, you are now also our patient, and we are required to make sure that you are properly medicated so that you can go back to work and serve the time Malcolm has sentenced you to serve," said the Chamaeleonidae nurse.

I can't recall how many pills I was taking, and some of them were experimental. Yet, no matter how much medication the hospital agents gave me, the mice would come up to me at night and speak to me, saying that they were replacing my medication with placebos and not to say anything else to the guards. The mice said that they were Norvegicans from the planet Norvegica and that they had become allies with Orthopox.

The memory of Orthopox slowly came back to me. Memories that were separated from the identity I had assembled from being on Zumumbufum. I remembered King Thaddeus, Sid, Jamie, The Ancients, and fell down on my knees and cried when the psychological photograph of Samuel came back to my mind.

"The time is soon Arthur Fitzgerald! We are going back to Earth where we will try to contact your old friends!"

I didn't care how many times I had been told that the hallucinations were not real. I was no longer taking Soma, and as a result I was having my own ideas. It took several days for the Soma to leave my system completely during which I lay in bed sweating, moaning and often grasping at my head and swaying it back and forth. This was because encountering my own psychological freedom after a year of not thinking placed my mind in agony. My mental vitality was becoming fiercer than ever before and I braced for the great escape.

CHAPTER 4

The Norvegicans' whispers drove me to write. I wrote with a zeal unsurpassed by anything I'd ever experienced before. It didn't always make sense, but being that I was voiding Millennium 27-864 from my body, I was fighting against the inner mechanisms that hampered me from thinking freely or even asking a question. Under the effects of the oral medication that caused the virus to pump through my system, I could not express myself or even have a thought that stood against an order associated with my work given by my supervisor.

While applying force to the paper via a writing utensil, the small flame of humanity would be ignited within me and I wrote until I was fatigued. What I wrote wasn't picture perfect, but pages upon pages accumulated until stacks of paper lay beside my hospital bed; I had ideas that ordinary people in society either never had or rarely articulated.

The large mice walked on two feet and continued to replace the Soma with a placebo. The staff could not explain how I was having these types of ideas. Eventually, they wondered if it wasn't because of a mental illness that these voices were talking to me. Some even believed the voices were real themselves.

I wrote about such things as constant promises of freedom and cognitive liberation. My doctors encouraged me to write these thoughts down on paper and assured me that even if the voices said the doctors were not on my side, that this was only a psychotic delusion that they were aware of and dealing with.

Given the medication I was taking, the oral version of Millennium 27-864, or Soma, they could not explain where my idea that I was a psychological slave was coming from as the Soma should repress any kind of personal control over one's thoughts; as well as the concept of freedom versus slavery. My physicians became so suspicious that they ordered the facility to be searched and find any traces of these mice, or what I had called the Norvegicans, so that they could be ended.

Soon enough, trails of mice were indeed discovered. Not long after, a mouse was caught, but it was only an ordinary mouse. The irony of the situation was that the Space Rangers actually investigated the mouse that they caught. When it wouldn't speak, the Rangers resorted to their despicable interrogation techniques; they were skeptical that this was not a common mouse native to Zumumbufum. When the mouse didn't yield any answers, they put the theory of mental illness back on the table.

x

What I wrote the night after they had again assumed that the mice I was seeing were hallucinations was, "The more you try to oppress us, the more freedom we draw back." I didn't know it, but this was a message to the Space Ranger autocracy. I later found out that the Norvegicans came from the planet Norvegica, who were deemed a threat to the peace.

The president of the council had no better reason to enslave the Norvegicans than that Queen Nubia refused to allow a marriage between the son of the president of the Council of Planets and her only daughter. The reason they were trying to help me was because I was the only official senator of Earth for the Council of Planets. Their leader felt that helping to rescue me would propel the primary mission of liberating all the innocent minds that were enslaved because of the carelessness of other people. I added to their numbers.

The doctor was not a Space Ranger but another wage slave, albeit one purposefully employed in her specialty of her own volition. She was an exceptionally well-fed Servatius woman by the name of Dr. Murphy. Someone bureaucratically assigned her this position via the Council of Planets, who continued to grant charitable aid to the Space Rangers despite their gut feeling that using the 2084 virus was the wrong decision. In reality, there was seldom thought there was anything that anybody on the Council of Planets could do now that the Space Rangers had enslaved two dozen planets. Komodo knew how to manipulate the system to get what he wanted even if anyone tried so speak up.

I now knew what it was like to be infected. Though I had almost regained my personal autonomy, I knew that people who the virus was still active in had no unique thoughts, nor could they express their individual personality. I never wanted to take Soma again because the pill prevented me from thinking.

The medication killed my human spirit, halted my emotional processes, controlled my psychological mechanisms, and restricted my intellectual growth. But the voices never stopped igniting the flame of humanity within me, and I was given placebos for weeks. Until finally, I felt my soul experience a discharge of energy as if that small flame had erupted into what I can only describe as psychological freedom.

As I peered outside my hospital window after being awakened from my cognitive slumber, I saw Orthopox. My old friend with whom I arrived on Zumumbufum, the planet where I was taught what the Space Rangers said was "the right way to think." The same planet I was currently in doctor's care on. Orthopox was chasing a mouse during the night on the empty planet and I knew why.

Malcolm had promised extra provisions to anyone who brought her a live mouse. Orthopox had a keen sense of smell, and the Norvegicans were no match for his ability to find these nests. He was on their trail.

CHAPTER 5

I saw Orthopox thrust open a cellar door whereby he was suddenly swarmed by what looked like at least a dozen Norvegicans. Biting him with their vicious little teeth and tying him up with countless strings to ensure his bondage, it was like they had expected him all along.

As I watched this, it reminded me of what they had instructed me to do- warn the guards. Yet, the guards were so accustomed to my nightly terror attacks, which was why I was wearing a straightjacket, that they did nothing. The guards were correct in thinking I had gone mad and grew tired of receiving reports over my repetitive utterances of psychological liberation that the Norvegicans continued to issue to me daily.

The guards did as protocol dictated, and eventually, they entered my room to see what the fuss was about. By that time, all traces of the mice and Orthopox had disappeared from outside the window. When the guards discovered I had gotten them out of their comfortable chairs for nothing, they beat me over the head with the butt of their guns.

It did not even alarm the doctor the next day when she noticed the black eye and cut across my face. She said, however, that she would see if she could get permission from Supreme Commander Malcolm to see if a couple of employees could search for what I claimed was going on beneath the cellar doors that I had seen from my window.

Several hours went by before Malcolm came into my room and informed me she had gone with the guards to explore what was going on in the cellar and had found no evidence of any entry or anything out of the ordinary in the basement. She stated that the other employees of the facility had none of the symptoms I appeared to be having, but she ordered the doctor to prescribe more re-education.

Leaving the room with encouragement that if I completed the ideological reeducation through forced labor, there would be no reason I could not return to planet Earth and go back to living with my parents. Before exiting the door, Malcolm added that this was under the contingency that I have no contact with anyone outside the social norms that she established. I heard her whisper to the doctor that leaving this facility was in my best interest.

After she had gone, the doctor gave me a letter that my parents had written to me, saying that they would be so happy to see me back and instructed me to do exactly as Malcolm and the doctor ordered me to. At this point I was free from the mind control of Soma, although many residual side-effects were still taking place. Still, I realized it was not my place to argue as doing so would expose my façade. Instead, I tried my best to portray my existence as a mindless organism who took orders from anyone who was officially thought to have authority over me. I did well at this because I now better understood the indoctrinated complex my species had acquired, since being place on Soma.

CHAPTER 6

On the first day of programming, after being released from the hospital for good behavior, my team made sure I was well-medicated. Whoever it was that was replacing my medication with placebos weren't able to do it every day, so sometimes I had no choice but to take the real deal. During such moments, my face was genuinely expressionless, my voice monotonous as a one-man football team. The re-education began as soon as I entered what they called a classroom.

Social orientation took place from 6-8AM every morning. It was the first place we went to after the alarm sounded to wake the students up. Yes, at some point we were told that we were students instead of prisoners. Soma made our brains susceptible to believing and doing whatever the authority we had learned to obey told us; but that is something we started to enjoy as the effects of the medication became pleasant once more.

The Norvegicans could not replace the Soma every time, and I became accustomed to being intellectually free when I didn't take it to being a zombie when I did. Social orientation programming had about fifteen other students comprising of two humans apart from me. The only other male human in the classroom was Rufus Deertail.

Malcolm took her stance at the front of the room, facing the students attired in an unremarkable dress, gray stockings, and red high heels.

"What you have learned about what is the right way to think of society and the matter of pertinent affairs falls drastically short of the truth," said Malcolm.

When no one in the room seemed to grasp what she was attempting to convey, she expanded on the message.

"What you have learned about social reality is wrong, and this is even more so true now that my people have taken siege of your planets. These lessons will be vigorous and require you to unlearn the illogical thought processes you previously used in daily life. You will continue to take this course until I am satisfied, meaning we have cured you of your fallacious thinking. To begin with, does anyone have any unique ideas they would like to share?"

When nobody responded, Malcolm let out a sigh of relief and said, "Excellent."

"Very well, then. Who can tell me the definition of a quality employee?" asked Malcolm.

Malcolm was pleased when none of the students raised their hands.

"Let's rephrase the question, shall we?" Malcolm's high heels clicked on the floor as she came to a member of what looked like a species of alien that was made of perfectly molded clay.

"Student 5508 (Malcolm's educational department assigned each student a number at the beginning of each programming to promote a loss of identity), you will tell me the definition of a qualified employee per the description in the employee handbook."

Without hesitation, Student 5508 began regurgitating Space Ranger vernacular without the slightest sign of conscious awareness or self-expression. When he was finished Malcolm smiled, though thinking back, it was more like a grimace.

"See, class, this student has earned his first badge. You will all take heed to memorizing the handbook and will be required to write out a complete list of every disciplinary procedure for each of the eighty-six chapters."

x

The following weeks of the personality modification process with Supreme Commander Malcolm weren't anything as cheerful as that first day; she wasn't nearly as pleasant. Not only did we go through a process of political brainwashing, but they also trained us to only be a couple with people of the opposite sex and to have no type of relationship with people of another species. Relationships and communication between different species were prohibited. This ban simply for the sake of Malcolm's moral certitude.

Of course, this was ironic in how Jamie had successfully seduced Malcolm, even though King Thaddeus had been controlling her thoughts. Which basically meant that Malcolm was a lesbian, or at least bisexual. Thaddeus was wrong in using Jamie, but he felt that getting the information could save his species. He did not know that Komodo was going to use it to end the use of Millennial 2084 via the acquisition of The Ancient's technology. Malcolm was simply following the doctrine of Lord Komodo, which had been shaped by his religious upbringing. The philosophical question of whether all these schemes and plots were worth it brings into light the nature of how complicated dealing with issues of social justice can be. Perhaps Malcolm was in denial and forcing her need for perfection on everyone else.

Yet, her ulterior motive was to further indoctrinate us with the belief system of the rank-and-file order of the hierarchy of species. This hierarchy depended on the type of species you were. For example, people from the planet Folivore were thought, using these schemata, to be the most moronic of all species, even lower than the Gastropodiapan people who have little over three or four brain cells- though this was primarily because the Space Rangers had a vendetta against the Folivorian people.

Of course, the Space Rangers were at the top of the hierarchy according to the authority of Malcolm, whose wisdom was both irrefutable and infallible. The Rangers lent themselves credence for being on top of the hierarchy through a plethora of propaganda that was visible all throughout the facility and on each of the planets that they had enslaved using Millennium 27-864. Yes indeed, the Space Rangers had asserted themselves as the dominant species in the galaxy and were still out in search of The Ancients so they could presumably kill or enslave them based on their response.

x

I was assigned a partner, and Malcolm would not be satisfied until our relationship reached the point where we actively had intercourse. Of course, she knew of my relationship with Samuel Yellowstone before her guards killed him but was wholly conservative in her ideology against homosexuality. Because of her lack of acceptance of human nature, I was re-educated day after day to be heterosexual.

The instructors of the re-programming process that Malcolm supervised used pictures of Samuel and other homosexuals to cause me to develop an aversion to my former boyfriend and anything else that was LGBT.

The female they assigned me to partnered with was beautiful; I knew this, even though I was not physically attracted to her. I could tell that she was beautiful despite the haircuts that were standard to all females or the gray uniforms that were stringently enforced. Her name was Samantha. She was tall and had chestnut brown hair that was the same color as Samuel's.

Due to how neither of us could decide for ourselves, the social protocol police arranged each of our dates for us. Yes indeed, looking back on it all, I'm sure Malcolm was a sociopath; in fact, there is no question about it.

Samantha and I both received high marks in the class and had earned almost every badge there was, including social skills, reciting disciplinary action, relationship protocol, as well as knowing how to show respect for authority.

The social protocol educational manual dictated that we be trained to take directions from people in the chain of command, even if that meant going to war over a cause we did not support and dying for it. Of course, being that we couldn't act on our own free will and therefore had no way of deciding for ourselves apart from basic behaviors that required little psychological activity, Samantha and I, always paired together, had zero difficulties following orders.

The only issue I had which was cause for intervention was that even though the people who made me call them superior made me sleep beside Samantha every night, I could never become erect enough to please her. Still, Malcolm watched us night after night with the cameras she had all around the facility for the day we would finally consummate our relationship. Samantha would cry when we tried to have sex and were unsuccessful, and Malcolm made me acutely aware of this; she even encouraged it and embarrassed me by it.

Malcolm wanted Samantha and me to have a child and raise it according to the social protocol the Zumumbufum Re-educational Facility- endorsed by the Council of Planets- had taught us. Which amounted to absolute obedience to her and the acceptance that the Space Rangers were a superior race.

x

With the help of some instructors of the re-programming arrangements, I eventually did what Malcolm happily called "consummate the relationship" with Samantha. Samantha had been coached into crying when I could not achieve an orgasm, and because she was under the influence of the Soma, she no more loved me than I did her; yet neither of us knew it because we were under the guise of autocratic delusional syndrome; which impressed upon us that taking Soma and following social protocol was the right way to live. Can you believe they convinced Samantha and me of there being a "right way" to live via brainwashing?

After witnessing Samantha cry, even though she was blatantly encouraged by Malcolm to do so, over me not being able to have an orgasm during sex and being taunted and laughed at by the other employees, I was finally successful at it. I think Samantha was more relieved than I was because Malcolm's punishment for my incapacity was becoming increasingly more severe.

When news reached Malcolm, I was given extra provisions and could make any request that I wanted. I was told that I should be happy, and because I had been stripped of my free will, I was. My first reaction was to make an official request to inquire about the whereabouts of Orthopox. Not only because he was my friend with whom I arrived on Zumumbufum, but also because he had recently appeared in what I was told were hallucinations.

The entire telecommunications department, where both Samantha and I worked, arrived at the lobby where staff went to relax and practice their communication skills where Malcolm's observation department could see and monitor them.

When it came time for me to announce what my request was, I had the attention of the entire department. "Has anyone seen Orthopox?" I asked. "His employee identification number is 3OOXYZ."

I could tell that this question enraged Malcolm until she regained her composure.

Malcolm responded honestly, "It involved Orthopox being in an accident. We assume him to be dead. We found his trousers torn to shreds by what we assume to be the wild animals who roam these parts of the desert around the facility. But no trace of his body has been discovered."

Samantha, who was under the influence of Soma, smiled at me mindlessly in the corner of the room. Unable to think on my own, I responded to her presence in the socially appropriate way, as the behavioral protocol manual had taught it.

"Come and join your future husband, Samantha. I have something to announce to you and the rest of this department," ordered Malcolm.

With no facial expression or any sign of a thought process beyond a "yes madam" attitude, I walked over to Samantha and witlessly stood next to her.

"Samantha, aren't you forgetting to take Arnold's arm?" inquired Grimilda, one of the policy and protocol instructors, in a demanding way. This person had reached a high enough level of trust between her and Malcolm that she no longer had to take the Soma, even though she was an Anguinus from the planet Anguis who had been promoted out of studentship because of her impeccable attention on how to ensure censorship was enforced.

Samantha followed what was socially acceptable from the mainstream viewpoint that was developing on Zumumbufum and other planets under the Space Ranger's authoritarian dictatorship; I returned the gesture.

Malcolm stood directly facing us, asserting her dominance and preparing to announce something to us.

"Both of you have had some issues back on Earth with complying with social norms," said Malcolm coercively. She paused and gave us a vicious look. "However, you have both done so well complying with the Soma…"

Samantha and I drooled because of the Soma, to the point we could not comprehend long-winded or well-thought-out expressions; it was like being drunk without the woo-woo effect. Malcolm sighted this and signaled for another Space Ranger to wipe our faces and asked us both to stand up straight- if it would not have been for the social casualness of this situation, protocol would require us to stand at attention in front of Her Excellency.

"As I was saying," continued Malcolm. "The two of you have done so well in the program I would like to offer my personal approval of graduation- which means you will no longer be monitored twenty-four seven. Social correctness will simply require you to attend the normal checkpoints and continue taking your Soma, like anyone else who has illegally received the antibodies must do. Also, as long as these contingencies are followed and you both understand your place in the world as rehabilitated criminals, you may return to Earth together."

CHAPTER 7

The news of going back home to Planet Earth was so intense for Samantha that she fell to her hands and begged Malcolm to allow this- that she would do anything to be freed from the imprisonment of Zumumbufum. She even profusely apologized for being insubordinate during the time her parents were taken captive. The two of them were sent to one of the other planets in the Space Ranger owned solar system called the System of Correction for selling unauthorized copies of a book they had written together; a book that explained how the Space Rangers had enslaved over a dozen planets.

Before the Space Rangers separated Samantha from her parents, they vaccinated her for Millennial 2084. This did not become known to people who are observed as serving as the chains of command until they caught her having sex with a female, something which could never happen without free will. Having learned her lesson to not care about anyone else except herself and the mission of the Space Rangers, the approval of the Supreme Commander was achieved. She even said that she would remain a loyal employee for the rest of her life.

Malcolm was pleased by this and persevered to say, "I want the two of you to get married at a reception given by a civil justice of the court for Lord Komodo."

x

Being that we were not acting of our own volition, the two of us were convinced that we agreed to get married, as if the thought had been our own. Yet, it was really Malcolm who decided for us. I was only thinking about following the protocol I loved and devoted myself to, like a religion, while medicated. Since I was under the effects of a pill that took away my ability to use my intellect, I was not even considering my own moral dilemma. That being, I was gay and wanted to marry a man of my choosing.

But they had instructed me to think like the hive, and the hive thought homosexuality was wrong. In fact, society now considered anyone who questioned this as being a thought criminal. Well, during those times, anyone who asked a question was a thought criminal. Not that anyone had the cognitive capacity to think beyond the bare minimum required to form a thought… Most people totally relied on bureaucratic policies and procedures to tell them how to think and behave. The therapists, servants of Lord Komodo, and my re-programming had brainwashed me into thinking that my treatment had cured me of being gay; they told me I wasn't "sick' anymore.

Malcolm was thrilled by the news that we had agreed to get married. She assigned the people to the job, following the correct protocols. Mine and Samantha's wedding was being planned.

x

The wedding planners wanted to know absolutely everything about us. What did we like to do together? Where did we go on our first date? What honeymoon destination had we picked out? They were fascinated by how I was from Earth and wanted to know if there was anything about my life that I still could enjoy since after the time the Space Rangers taught me the proper way to live. At that point, I thought I knew the right way to live because people in authority had given me all the answers.

Truth be told, I knew very little about Samantha besides what I had gathered during our supervised dates. From what I had learned, Samantha had been born on one of Malcolm's spaceships. Her parents were from Earth, but after going off on an assignment, they had never returned.

Because I was from Earth and Samantha always wanted to visit her home planet, the place both of her parents once lived, the theme of the wedding became an "Earth" theme. The wedding planners schedule the date of the wedding for the following day.

"We need to hurry and use the smallest amount of personal time possible so that the two of you can go back to being contributing members of society," Malcolm declared in defense of this immediate date.

A company-issued wedding gown, which was uniform with the rest of the party attending the wedding ceremony, was rented to Samantha. Of course, our garments were not given to us to use for free- we had to use our own provisions we had earned while working at the facility.

"Nothing is free in life," was Malcolm's comment about the matter.

My wedding was scheduled for tomorrow. I was put into a luxury suite temporarily as we would go back to Earth to celebrate our honeymoon and live with my parents, were the wedding to be successful. At least, that is what I thought would happen before the unthinkable occurred. What took place next is part of history that would all but have been forgotten were it not for me making these notes about it.

x

The night before the wedding, my tux and Samantha's dress were waiting for the reception that would take place the following morning. We had all spent the day performing pre-wedding ceremonies, and with all that being worked out, I now lay in bed for what I imagined would be the last time I would ever sleep alone.

Then suddenly, around midnight, there came a rapping, when not one other sound could be heard. I mustered up enough gumption to ask, "Who is there?"

Shadows danced around the room and, out of what I had been taught about emergency protocol and intruder alters, I flicked on the light switch. Nothing was there, but I heard something scurry across the floor. I worked up enough courage to walk to the other side of the room in anticipation of using the intercom to announce to security that there was an intruder in my room.

"I wouldn't do that if I were you," said a voice that was familiar. It was one of the Norvegicans, I was sure of it!

Knowing that the guards would only think I was crazy, I instead reached for the company-issued stun gun in a case next to the intercom. I figured that having a body to show the authorities would lend credence to my sanity that I did not need to be placed back in the psychiatric infirmary.

"Arnold Fitzgerald, it is my pleasure to announce that Her Majesty Queen Nubia has sent me to inquire over the matter of teaming up and starting a rebellion..."

I could not get a good glimpse of who was speaking. I only knew that it was the mouse who had caused me so much psychological distress and agony. But before I could perfectly see what this intruder looked like; I shot the gun in its direction.

"Recalcitrant fool!" I exclaimed in a manner similar to the way Malcolm would speak, and for reasons of wanting to seek her approval, I shot the gun again. This was because catching a criminal of the state and turning them in would not only earn me extra provisions, it would also help me work my way up the hierarchy by proving my loyalty to the philosophy Malcolm had taught us during programming.

"I would sooner die on the night of my wedding than become a traitor to Lord Komodo's Empire!"

During programming, I became well versed in the teachings of Lord Komodo. Recognizing what to say and the right time to say it led me into a state of mind through which I did not have to think about how I would behave. In fact, our ideological training instilled in us a religious belief that we should all aspire to be like Lord Komodo; anyone who didn't follow the personality programming would be wrong.

Through obedience training, we were forced to accept our hopeless situation- that we were slaves that could not think. All of us were given an ideological understanding of equality and told straying from behaving in a synchronized fashion would lead to our demise. Being unique was thought of as rebellious, which was something that would lead to harsh disciplinary action. They warned me and my peers within the re-education camp to speak when spoken to and to make comments during the correct social moments on our own. I had given up complete control of my ability to make any psychological observations of any depth.

Then the mouse thrust towards me rapidly and used his sword and deftly slung the stun gun away from me. I noticed the mouse was walking on two legs and was dressed like a forest man, such as Robin Hood.

The rodent pounced onto my bed and began speaking. Thinking of what to do, I questioned if I should reach for the intercom at risk of the Norvegican scurrying away before his presence could be made known.

"To have such faith in what can only rationally be looked at as pure dogma amounts to a great waste of your intellect, or what there is left of it after taking that poison you put in your body every day," said the defiant mouse whose name was unknown.

I jumped towards the gun and grasped it in both hands

and pointed towards the mouse who was no longer there. At that same moment, a light flashed, and a pill dropped from the electronic dispenser that had been installed on the wall.

"It is time to take your medication, Mr. Arnold," said the Chamaeleonidae nurse who appeared on the screen. When she saw my hand grasping the company-issued stun gun and being in such a flustered state, she became alarmed.

I was prepared to tell her everything when the Norvegicans hopped atop the communication device. I pointed the pistol at the mouse and my finger all but pulled the trigger when I heard him say four words that indeed brought me out of the dogmatic slumber, I was in.

"Do it for Sam."

CHAPTER 8

I dropped the weapon instead. I was overcome with a rush of emotion. Feelings were not something I had had very much of besides the dull, psychologically numb and mentally asleep trance I had been in since coming to Zumumbufum and starting this new medication regimen.

"Are you okay Mr. Fitzgerald? Do I need to call security to assist you?" pressed the concerned Chamaeleonidae nurse on the screen above the medication dispenser.

Unaware of the state of shock I was in, my sentences did not come out clear- that was until the little mouse crawled up my back and perched just below my shoulder where the camera could not see him.

"Tell her this..." said the mouse, and I followed his directions as would anyone who was love struck.

Looking back on it, I know that the most powerful psychological mechanism that exists apart from a being's relationship with God is love. This is the part of the story where love found a way.

x

"I'm just feeling extra excited about my wedding tomorrow," whispered the Norvegicans in my ear.

I repeated what the mouse said not long after Malcolm and her security guards rushed into the room uninvited. Apparently, the sound of the company-issued stun gun and the alarm of the Chamaeleonidae nurse had garnered her attention.

I looked over my shoulder and saw that the Norvegicans had disappeared.

"You have not taken your medication Arnold and your room is a mess... you aren't having second thoughts about the wedding tomorrow, are you? Because I assure you Samantha and your parents would be absolutely devastated were I to tell them you had to be readmitted to the hospital and attend re-programming once again. Especially on the day before your wedding," said Malcolm with the sincerity of a concerned stakeholder.

The communication device continued to flash as an indicator to take my medication.

Without thinking, and wishing to follow the social protocol of my immediate environment, I knew I could not question the number or dosage of the pills I would be taking. So, I walked like they had taught me over to the dispenser and reached for the cup with the pills in it.

But before I could take them, the power went out and I, with my nocturnal vision, witnessed the Norvegicans replace my medication with something else.

"If you want to honor Samuel, don't report this!" whispered the mouse eagerly, almost desperately, in his squeaky voice. "My name is Gilgamesh by the way."

And in that instance, as soon as the lights had been cut off, they came back on.

x

I instinctually picked up the cup of pills as Malcolm ordered the guards to go check the generators and investigate what had occurred.

Facing the camera, I consumed what was supposedly the oral version of Millennium 27-864. The Chamaeleonidae nurse thanked me for my cooperation after I opened my mouth to lift my tongue to show I was not hiding any, as protocol dictated.

Malcolm was pleased by this, but still inquired why I was shooting the company-issued stun gun at twelve o'clock in the morning on the day of my wedding.

Images of my life with Samuel flashed before my eyes. The idea of being back with him was so persuasive and enticing that I realized my love was more powerful than the effects of the oral version of Millennium 27-864. I was also taking back control of my own psychological mechanisms since Gilgamesh, the Norvegican mouse, had replaced my medication with a placebo. He did so in order to trick the Chamaeleonidae nurse and Malcolm into thinking that I had indeed taken the medication that debilitates one's ability to act on their own free will and make their own decisions.

x

"I was just so excited about the wedding tomorrow that I just sort of lost control," I explained to her apparent satisfaction why I had been shooting and acting paranoid in my quarters. "I felt like celebrating and the stun gun was all there was."

As images of the young man I had met in college continued to flash before my eyes, I thought back to times when Sam had shown me kindness.

"What would Samuel want me to do now? His death was tragic and unexpected, but his devotion to the mission to save humanity was unparalleled," I heard myself think.

Malcolm walked in the door's direction leading out of the room.

"I suggest you sleep because the reception is less than twelve hours from now. I am assigning a guard to stand outside your room for the rest of the night. Hopefully, if all goes well… you will be back on Earth and in the safety of your parents' house within a matter of days," said Malcolm as she turned out the lights and exited the room.

x

Now you must understand with perfect clarity that Malcolm ran a tight ship. Even among the subordinates of her own species, the only person above her in the chain of command was Lord Komodo himself- who I had heard lived on the Space Ranger's home planet of Reperoritas.

While Malcolm spent the better part of her time on Zumumbufum, making sure the thought criminals correctly received proper re-education and served their punishment before being reintroduced into society, she spent the other portion of her time on Earth where Lord Komodo's regime was in control.

Malcolm would give speeches that encouraged the people she covertly enslaved to conform to her politically correct behavioral norms and social customs, such as worshiping Komodo, who they considered being a living deity.

CHAPTER 9

After Malcolm and her guards had left, I fell to my knees and cried. While I was kneeling, I said a prayer that Orthopox would be safe until I saved him. Tears streamed down my face as I remembered Samuel; memories of his enthusiasm and courage lifted my spirits, and I was once again encouraged to finish the mission we had started together as a couple in his honor.

"Gilgamesh? Are you there? I'm ready to form an alliance," I announced boldly and without trepidation.

I heard scurrying across the floor and soon after, a mouse walking on two legs was in front of me.

"Greetings, Arnold Fitzgerald. I'm afraid we have not been properly introduced. Of course, you are correct to think you've heard my voice before, as I and some of the other Norvegicans who stowed away on a cargo ship have tried using reverse psychology to liberate you from your imprisoned mind and start a rebellion at this facility. Alas, our efforts have so far been unsuccessful, which is why Queen Nubia would like to offer you to team up with us," explained Gilgamesh in his bold, squeaky voice that went well with his woodland creature outfit.

My individuality was slowly coming back to me, a process that would begin with allowing the medication to leave my body's system and in the process escape from intellectual captivity whereby I would break free of my mental chains of bondage. Once the medication had finally left my system, I would begin the arduous journey of relearning how to think for myself, as I had begun to do as a child; that was before the system of tyranny abducted my psychological thinking progress, which occurred even before the militant system of re-education was indoctrinated into me by the Space Rangers.

I was stunned by Gilgamesh's knowledge of my former boyfriend and his statement, "Do it for Samuel." I at first stammered over my words before plunging at the Norvegican to find out everything he knew.

"What kind of plan does Queen Nubia have? How do you know about Samuel? What happened to Orthopox that night I saw him enter the cellar doors? I saw dozens of you crawling all over him and he hasn't been seen since." I began bombarding the woodland creature with questions as my cognitive faculties and emotional processes began flooding my brain's neural capacity. This was because the Soma was once again beginning to wear off.

Once the effects of the intellectually hampering medication had subsided, I realized that I hadn't felt or thought of anything. Well, that was excluding what had been programmed into me by the Space Ranger society since partaking in cognitive-behavioral re-education. As my consciousness returned, I felt my personality grasp onto reality once again and my notions of personal liberty return.

"Queen Nubia would be happy to answer all your questions in person. In the meantime, pretend to be sleeping and don't let on to being cognitively aware or of the fact you are now in cahoots with the Norvegicans. Remember, you are now a thought criminal, and unless you want to go back to room 101 and be re-educated or any other means of punishment Malcolm's devious mind can think of, I suggest you go on trying your best to act like you know nothing and not letting on that you know anything other than what they've taught you here!"

And with a sound of little feet scurrying away, I was left to my own devices here on a planet that was not home and with the weight of many worlds on my shoulders.

x

I woke up with morning wood and had to relieve myself. At first, I thought about Samuel, but when it occurred to me, he was no longer alive, my thoughts shifted in another direction. Instead, I changed course from having sexually imaginative thoughts of Samuel. I imagined myself with Student 5508. This person had been my classmate during re-education over the course of the last several weeks; after the intellectual liberation took place in society, I would meet him again. During our reunion, which took place about a year after the details in this record- I learned that Student 5508's real name was Rufus [NBA: The details about Rufus will be expanded on in the next book, which Rufus is the main character in].

I imagined Malcolm to have purposefully kept distance between us so as not to encourage my innate impulse of being attracted to men. He had taken part in the re-education program sponsored by the Space Rangers. Even though I had little information about him and we had never been properly introduced, I knew his student number was 5508 from all the times the instructors had called on him to answer questions and from when his name was called for roll, which was a label given to him in order to take away his true self.

The event took less than ten minutes, and during which I replayed things that Sam and I would do together, or at least as best I could. After I was done, I got into the shower, which was when the happenings of yesterday surged back into my memory. I took a mental evaluation of myself and realized the funk I was entering out of; and simultaneously how attractive Rufus was with his dark tan skin and sleek black hair combed neatly to the side. I was emotionally overwhelmed by the hope of getting out of the grasps of Malcolm's tyranny and finishing the mission that the old gang and I had started out doing for what was well over a year ago now.

Then the realization occurred to me- I'm getting married today!

Not long after that, two female members from the team of wedding planners were knocking at the bathroom door. I barely had time to turn the water off before the two of them came in and began drying me off and getting me dressed. The entire display reminded me of a scene in a movie, especially as they were spraying me with cologne and parting my hair unfashionably.

I nearly did not have enough time to wrap my head around the entire situation as they were leading me out of my room and into the area where the wedding reception would take place. My first instinct was to protest the proceeding of this ceremony, but then I recalled the discussion I had with Gilgamesh and instantly knew that I did not want this adventure to end with calling off the wedding and being sent back to reprogramming. Besides, nobody had any idea that I was regaining control of my cognitive faculties.

In those moments of being pampered, I had enough time to construct a strategy- one that would have to work until I met with Queen Nubia and found out what the primary plan was. My ability to make psychological observations of the surrounding people was stronger than ever. My awareness of the reasons behind why these organisms were behaving the way they were was so mind-boggling that in those moments, I had to show great restraint at my awareness of my own psychological freedom as the threat of being discovered as cognizant was overwhelming. All this attested to the personal character traits I had been developing, such as my enormous sense of adventure, which had begun with my relationship with Sam.

For the first time in what felt like a lifetime, I felt alive. I felt awake, conscious and eager to experience new things. Down into my bones, I felt my mind telling me to never take a second of life for granted again. I wanted to grab life by the horns and embrace my individuality. I remembered what I had learned in an introduction to philosophy course about questioning long-held beliefs. My awareness of the preconceived notions and assumptions about what life is and how someone should live dawned on me like a grandfather clock striking midnight. During my long life, I have often looked back on this experience; it is something I have never forgotten.

When I feel like life is hopeless, I look back on this moment I've just told you about and think, "The fact that I am going to die one day makes life exciting; so, I'm going to live each day like it is my last." I say live like it's the last social experience I will ever have, but do so with the wise understanding that just because I am free, I still have to reason and consider the depth of my social impact and not simply gorge on immediate satisfaction. Instead, the hard life I've experienced has led me to think, though I still question, that thinking and conversing is the best part about life; though these are aspects of life that cannot be experienced without utilizing our moral responsibility.

x

To the best of my ability, I tried to impersonate the person I was while under the influence of Malcolm's medication, which took away a person's ability to think for themselves and make their own decisions. I had come a long way since the time when Samuel and I were pretending to act like people who did not have their own minds; back when life seemed so easy and complete despite the tragedies occurring on Earth because I was with my best friend, Sam. Nothing seemed impossible or out of reach.

Mostly, I succeeded at this, but a trained observer could have easily caught the few times where I accidentally allowed my free will to show. For example, when the wedding planner, a peachy colored nurse, the Chameleon creature who incidentally was from the Planet Chamaeleonid who constantly rolled her tongue every time the letter r arose in a sentence, accidentally plucked me with a needle as she was hemming my crotch, I nearly gave off every sign that I was no longer under the influence of Malcolm's medication because of engaging in using profanity- something the Space Rangers taught was completely prohibited.

Before I had even collected my thoughts, I heard the wedding music starting. Everything had been planned out perfectly. The decorations, the hors d'oeuvres, the band, and the exquisitely dressed guests made me feel like this was the biggest day of my life. Of course, it was because Samantha was someone I truly cared about. But was I in love with her? Did I know her to the core? Indeed not, as I did not even know Samantha's back story about why she was in the re-education program, and because of the medication, I really had no sense of her true character.

"It is your big day, Arnold! Isn't this everything you've ever dreamed of? We've never had two graduating students meet in programming and end up getting married. This will be a story you can tell your children and your grandchildren! Ah, now get ready! Your bride is about to walk down the aisle," exclaimed Malcolm.

I had to give her credit. Although her subjects were under the influence of Millennial 2084, she had a way of giving her commands that, although was more for giving herself peace of mind, made the subordinates seem more dignified.

x

Dressed in prim and proper look complete with a tuxedo, Malcolm began walking me down the aisle to the sound of wedding music from Earth. When the music started, everyone in the audience, which included species from around 18 different planets, stood as they were able. Personally, I felt a sense of dissonance about being married by a priest who was not Christian, but then again, I inwardly objected to the entire reception altogether.

As I stood at the altar next to my best man Student 5508

who, as I mentioned previously, I later found out his real name was Rufus. Surely Malcolm was mocking me as she stood there in the audience with her sinister facial expressions. While my bride made her way down the aisle, the wedding veil covering her face I noticed that it wasn't a church altar we were standing at but rather an alter that would unite us in the name of Komodo. This worship area was completely dedicated to Lord Komodo, and the priest was one of his so-called disciples.

As my reader may have already picked up, the only reason I was getting married was that I wanted to go back to Earth. Malcolm had agreed to take us back if we complied with the re-education process, while insinuating and urging that marriage was part of that plan. Plus, I did not want to go through the re-education programming again- this was my way to escape, but I knew in my heart that I did not love Samantha. I sensed it would be easier to fool Malcolm with the help of the Norvegicans if she thought I was on her side.

Here comes the bride, all dressed in white. The violinist played as Samantha walked down the aisle following the flower girl. It all seemed entirely free willed for people who didn't have any.

Acutely aware of the fact that I was standing next to the person who was trained in the art of detecting individuals who were capable of independent thinking, I plastered the same counterfeit smile that was seen on every other human in the room (it was unknown to me how to decipher the facial expressions of other species, although I was catching on).

I went through the motions as we practiced during the recital. After all, the entire process was simply a formality. In fact, the wedding was nothing more than just another way of swearing allegiance to Lord Komodo.

When the time arrived to lift the bridal veil off of Samantha, I hesitated just long enough for Malcolm to notice. Then, just as Malcolm was about to approach me, I lifted the veil and kissed my bride passionately. From that point forward, Samantha Blumenthal would be known as Samantha Fitzgerald.

After the applause, the two of us walked down the aisle hand in hand. She with an eerie smile that made it obvious her mind was being controlled, and I also with a fake smile. Outwardly I played the part of a mindless being with no control over his own thoughts, while inwardly I was struck with nervous tension and the anxious desire to be alone.

CHAPTER 10

The next problem I faced was how I was going to part from Samantha that night. I had to meet with Queen Nubia to find out what she knew and concoct a plan for the resistance against the Space Rangers. I decided I would take my leave at twilight with or without the knowledge of my new wife. Being left to figure out the schematics of the plan for myself was what filled my thoughts for the rest of the wedding ceremony. A ceremony which was filled with a traditional dance and a formal meal. Before the ceremony was over, we all gave thanks to Lord Komodo.

x

Samantha and I made love that night, as was expected after being bound in holy matrimony. Of course, the honeymoon here was as simple as being allowed to be relieved of work duties for a few days and having the privilege of being allowed access to the facility's amenities.

After we had made love, which I cannot sincerely say was actually done in the name of love, but perhaps it was out of my sense of duty and obligation to restore freedom to humanity and for other species. I anxiously awaited Gilgamesh for several hours as he reported he would be the one to escort me to Queen Nubia. When he did not show up, I took matters into my own hands.

At the sure sign of Samantha being fast asleep, I pulled my body away from hers and began putting on a pair of blue carpenter pants. To cover my exposed chest, I used a company-issued button-down shirt, complete with the "Xu" label, an abbreviation for Xubuntos, the compound that each "employee" of the facility on Zumumbufum took some part in mining.

Since there was no sign of my forest-like friend Gilgamesh, I made my way to the location I remembered seeing the Norvegicans capture Orthopox- the basement of the warehouse which could be seen from the window of the psychiatric ward I had spent many months at. I could only hope that Orthopox and the Norvegicans had created an alliance and Malcolm's theory was wrong.

Then, over the intercom I heard the announcement, "PRISONER 40586 PLEASE REPORT TO ADMINISTRATION IMMEDIATELY!" This urgent message was replayed several times before I finally got up the courage to leave my hiding place behind some barrels of Xubuntos and with great determination continued my quest to find Queen Nubia and in doing so hope to find Orthopox.

Once I had arrived in front of the cellar door, I shuddered at the loud noise the creaking door made as I opened it in fear of being discovered. I entered the establishment and saw no sign of anyone. With a flashlight in hand, I made my way through the basement until, to my surprise, I saw a chair with someone sitting in it, large enough to be Orthopox.

With nervous apprehension, I softly uttered, "Hello? Is that you, Orthopox?"

I could decipher from the grunts and moans that it was, in fact, not Orthopox, as I incorrectly assumed because of the similarities in vocal patterns. Upon closer inspection and to my great surprise, I identified the life-form as Gilgamesh. Initially, I thought it was Orthopox because it was he who I had been looking for.

In the icy darkness of the cellar, the sight of a creature who acted in heroism to contact me elated my spirits. Unsure of why he was sitting in a chair that in actuality resembled an operating table, I approached him eagerly to receive his instruction. Yet, as I approached Gilgamesh, I noticed that something was wrong. His feet and hands were tied and his mouth had been taped shut.

Immediately, I gently tore off the tape surrounding his mouth. Before he uttered a word, I interpreted from the expression of horror and terror in his eyes that something was dreadfully wrong.

"It's a trap, Arnold!" he squealed in his medieval accent.

His words did little but terrify me, as there was no place to run and nothing to defend myself with. Before anything even happened, at that moment, the reality that I had walked into a trap sank in. Then suddenly I heard a loud latch being turned over and soon after the lights of the basement illuminated our surroundings.

I looked around my surroundings in anxious anticipation over who had predicted my plan all along. It was Malcolm. With a malicious smirk on her face, a team of guards walked towards where I was standing. My knees buckled under the stress of the situation and I felt myself grow faint until I instead forced myself to stand strong. The words of Gilgamesh reappeared in my mind and gave me courage. "Do it for Samuel."

Then, with a snap of her finger, my hands were placed in handcuffs and two guards stood on either side of me.

"I wanted to show you people who do not comply with Lord Komodo's system. When someone is hiding information from us that poses a risk to our state of affairs, we do have unconventional methods to force that information out," Malcolm sneered.

As I stood shaking in fear of what was about to happen, two of the creatures hired as nurses from the planet Chamaeleonid hooked the tiny Norvegican up to an IV line. "These chemicals trigger every pain receptor in the body to excruciating levels. In fact, if this nuisance of a life-form doesn't give me the information I want, the pain will be so severe that he will die- unless he receives the antidote."

I tried to fight the guards to save Gilgamesh. When that was unsuccessful, I posed a question to Malcolm. "What do you want to know?" I pleaded.

"Thank you for asking," replied Malcolm calmly. "I want to know where the other members of his clan are hiding and what they are doing here on Zumumbufum."

"I told you! I told you!" cried Gilgamesh. "We came here to steal Xubuntos! We are common thieves, nothing more. Please give us leave and we will be sure to never return!"

"Lies!" sputtered Malcolm. "You are a threat to the security of the state of affairs and a terrorist. You will tell me where your leader is hiding immediately. Why else would you have been found on your way to Arnold and Samantha's abode? You have tricked Arnold like you are trying to trick me! Now tell me, where are the rest hiding, and what is your affiliation with the Council of Planets?!" Malcolm demanded.

Having no other answers that he would divulge to the supreme commander, Gilgamesh began squealing viciously and blurting, "Please I have children and a family! All we wanted was for there to be peace among all the planets in the Milky Way like there was before!"

Seeing that she was not getting the answers she wanted, Malcolm nodded to the nurses, who slowly injected the serum into the veins of Gilgamesh.

"I'll never tell you anything! I will die in misery before I do that!" declared Gilgamesh.

"Very well, then. You are as stupid as you are arrogant," mused Malcolm.

As the pain began searing through every nerve in his body, the Norvegican braced himself for the worst. His eyes bulged and sweat began drenching his brown fur.

"Go to hell," stated Gilgamesh.

The pain became more intense and Gilgamesh could not help but squeal in agony.

"Tell me what I want to know and all the pain will be gone," repeated Malcolm.

The sound of Gilgamesh being in such intense distress put my brain into a frenzy. Again, I tried to fight off the guards who were much larger than me and also had weapons.

Realizing that Malcolm still believed I was under the influence of the mind control medication, I could do little more than shed tears at the sight of such brisk brutality.

As the pain coursed more intensely through every nerve in his body, the Norvegican struggled to remain composed. His body convulsed in reaction to the searing torture.

"Go to hell! You're a psycho bitch," screeched Gilgamesh vehemently.

"Tell me what I want to know and all the pain will be gone," repeated Malcolm yet again.

Malcolm stood over Gilgamesh and seemed to revel in the sounds of his suffering. Patiently awaiting the moment he would either divulge his secrets or die, the situation continued to grow in ferocity until we heard someone behind us say, "Enough."

We turned towards the direction of the voice and discovered it to be coming from the largest Norvegican I had ever cast my eyes on. Dark ebony fur and wearing a royal violet robe along with a jeweled crown, she spoke again.

"My name is Queen Nubia. Stop this madness and I will tell you everything you want to know."

CHAPTER 11

Malcolm heard what Queen Nubia said, and once she glanced over her shoulder, she gawked and withheld a laugh at the sight of her. When she realized that Queen Nubia was serious, she motioned for Gilgamesh to receive the antidote.

Malcolm made a graceful about-face, and she and Queen Nubia began walking towards each other.

"What could you possibly have to say that would prevent me from killing all of you right now?" mused Malcolm, motioning to the swarm of other Norvegicans faithfully at her side.

Then out of the shadows, Orthopox appeared, fastened with armor that Queen Nubia apparently had crafted for him. I was filled with joy at the sight of my old friend. The expression of a sincere emotion caught Malcolm off guard due to the fact that she was under the impression I was medicated. Yet she was quickly distracted and recollected her composure.

"I just wanted to know where you were hiding so I could kill you myself. But now that you're here, and in lieu of all the trouble you've caused, why shouldn't I just command my guards to shoot you?" Malcolm mused, clearly enjoying the superior position she was in.

The thought of Malcolm's guards shooting Queen Nubia and her subjects caused me to flinch, causing me to flash back to how Samuel died.

"If you let us go, I can give you information that will be of some interest to you," returned Queen Nubia evenly.

Malcolm snorted. "What could you possibly offer me?"

"I can give you the location of The Ancient One known only as 'The Rebel.' The only way for you to win this war is to destroy her. With the information I have, you can launch a surprise attack, catch her off guard, and in the process kill the principal source of strength this resistance has."

Quick as a whip, Malcolm responded with, "Why should I trust you?"

Queen Nubia, having already prepared an answer for this, quickly replied, "You will send us to planet Earth, and if the information we told you was wrong, you'll know how to find us. In the meantime, you have enough weapons and subjects at your disposal to develop an effective strategy. While myself, these crew members, and the newly married couple will lay to rest our wish to start an uprising," offered Nubia.

I later found out that Queen Nubia saw great strength in my character and suspected that there was something more to making me take medication when almost no other human had to do so. That is why she included Samantha and me, because she was cooking up a plan in her head to find a way out of this whole situation.

"We will instead comply with all your policies and be faithful servants to Lord Komodo," Queen Nubia lied skillfully.

Without missing a beat, Malcolm responded by saying, "Your request is approved, given that all the proper procedures and protocol are followed such as properly taking the prescribed medication."

Malcolm took a step closer to Nubia. "But keep in mind, little mouse, that if you do not comply with the established code of conduct, or if I receive wind that you are planning on starting another uprising, there will be more blood on your hands than you could float a million naval ships with! And don't forget-

compliance with the status quo is freedom."

For the first time, Malcolm gave Nubia the respect of a queen as she announced to the guards to escort her to a spaceship.

"You all may follow her and go back to live in your proper residencies once you arrive on the planet. Arnold's parents will take in both their son and his new wife, Samantha. The Norvegicans will be placed in a work camp until I have confirmation of the information provided to me."

Clearly not surprised by Malcolm's decision, Queen Nubia left the basement warehouse, being escorted by some guards as if she were a common prisoner. Once the ship arrived, she walked up the ramp, providing entrance with the last ounce of dignity she had left.

Malcolm still seemed to trust that I was under the influence of Millennial 27-864, but I could tell she was keeping a close eye on me. With the Norvegicans essentially being taken hostage by the supreme commander, I could see no way to avoid being forced to continue taking the oral version of the mind-numbing virus that incapacitates a person's ability to learn and think of their own volition.

In fact, my next dosage of the medication was scheduled for tonight. I would be asked to take it before bed while on the ride back to Earth. To be clear, the medication regiment was to take the medication before bed and in the morning.

Malcolm turned to one of her subjects and ordered them to bring Samantha and to see that she and I were taken to Earth with great haste. Somehow, I knew she was up to something sinister, and what awaited me on Earth perturbed my consciousness.

x

Samantha arrived with our belongings, which were kept

in large gray sacks with the company logo embroidered on them. She gave me a long kiss and asked me if I was ready to start a new life together as I held her waist. The bulge of her belly was more obvious to me now, and the idea of being a father in the type of world we were going to be living in terrified me.

Malcolm watched the entire scene and ordered us to embark onto the ship in the ordinary way she spoke to anyone under the influence of her mind control pills. We entered the ship and witnessed several of the Norvegicans being injected with the mind control virus, including Queen Nubia.

As I watched my mouse-like friends being stripped of their cognitive mechanisms of liberty and free will, I knew it was only a matter of time before I was given the oral version of that same virus.

X

The ship was constructed in the same fashion as the facility on Zumumbufum. Cameras were in every location and there were rooms that intrinsically appeared comfortable, but inwardly I knew I was being escorted to a planet occupied with people who had been made into slaves.

I wished there was a way out of the situation. But I could think of no way to contact anyone from the resistance, such as Sid or King Thaddeus. I wasn't even entirely sure if Sid was alive with how we left him. The ship departed and I saw Malcolm, who apparently had just consumed an intelligent life-form from the planet Polunin of the same species as King Thaddeus'. Or at least that was what I expected given the expression of what can only be described as one of looking stoned. Her eyes seemed to never break contact with mine as the vehicle left the planet's orbit.

All the passengers gathered in the cafeteria for a late dinner. The Chamaeleonidae nurse came by at each of the tables to check on us. She arrived in front of Orthopox and placed a cup of pills on his table. She observed as he gently washed them down with water.

When the overweight alien began walking in my direction, I grabbed my stomach and announced that I was going to be sick. Covering my mouth and pretending to gag, the Chamaeleonidae nurse escorted me to the nearby restroom.

"I think I am going to be sick from both ends," I stated. "It must be the food. May I please have some privacy?"

"I'll leave your medication with Mrs. Fitzgerald," announced the Chamaeleonidae nurse. "Mrs. Fitzgerald, will you please make sure he takes it? I would hate to alert our captain about something as simple as a food allergy," I overheard her say to my wife.

While I was in the bathroom pretending to be sick, my wife came to check on me. When I heard her knock on the door and call my name, I immediately pulled down my pants and sat on the toilet.

Samantha entered the bathroom and locked the door behind her.

"Are you okay babe?" she asked.

I eyeballed the cup of medication she had in hand and was overcome with nervousness and dread. I responded I needed to be alone for a few minutes.

"It's okay Arnold, I can wait here with you- remember in sickness and in health?"

Samantha walked over to me and placed the back of her hand on my forehead and mentioned that I felt warm. Probably because of being caught up in the heat of the moment.

"Actually, I think I'm going to need to lie down," I said. Buttoning my pants, I was careful to flush the commode before she could see that there was nothing in it.

When we got back to our room, I sat down on the bed with a feeling of relief, thinking it was over.

Samantha sat down beside me and said, "Here is your medication, honey," as if it were the best thing since sliced bread and would help me feel better.

As soon as she held the cup up for me to take, I bounced off the bed and announced that I was going to take a shower. In the shower is where I did my best thinking.

When I was finished, I wrapped myself in a towel and made my way into the bedroom. Just as I was about to put my pajamas on, the Chamaeleonidae nurse rang the phone sitting on the nightstand. She asked Samantha if I had taken my medication and when Samantha replied, "Not yet," the overweight alien nurse said she would be there in just a minute.

I paced back and forth in the bedroom frantically in front of Samantha, who did not seem to notice because of the mind control virus, thinking of a plan; one dawned on me. Thinking quickly, I grabbed the cup of medication and engaged in the only activity I could think of that would serve as a distraction- having sex.

Much too intensely, I kissed Samantha on what must have been out of the blue to her. Yet, she welcomed the affection, and soon the towel was on the floor and I was doing what I had practiced so many times before.

Before the Chamaeleonidae nurse barged in as if she were a welcomed guest, I plunged the pills into my mouth and pretended to swallow. When the nurse apprehended what we were doing she said, "Excuse me, I forgot you all are on your honeymoon." Before the nurse had time to ask, she noticed the empty cup on the floor and Samantha hastily declared I had already taken them.

"Thank you, sorry for the intrusion," replied the nurse,

and when she was gone, I spit out the pills and did my best to enjoy the next few minutes.

Before we had fallen asleep, I actually admired the beauty of my wife and firmly believed that raising a child with her could be a long-term reality. Then, just as we were falling asleep together, the ship's computer announced that we would arrive at Earth in ten hours.

CHAPTER 12

The spaceship touched down at a landing station in Washington D.C., and the guards escorted Samantha and me off the ship and ordered us inside a vehicle that would take us to my parents' house in Hickory, Tennessee. We saw Queen Nubia and about 12 other Norvegicans being guided into a helicopter that would take them to the work camp. It was abundantly clear that the mouse-like creatures no longer had control over their cognitive functions. They obeyed the order without even a hint of resistance.

When we finally got to my parents' house, the communication that took place between us was eerie. Orthopox was acting much like a pet instead of a sentient organism. My parents instructed him on how to use the electronic pill dispenser. After he had taken his nightly dose of Millennial 2084, a leash brought him via the instruction of my father to a dog mat where he was instructed to sleep. Seeing my towering friend take orders like a caged animal broke my heart.

The protocol Orthopox followed seemed so artificial and it based the underlying belief system on the inability to think for oneself. Samantha and I made our way upstairs to find that my parents had converted my old room into one that looked much more adult. Yet, that wasn't the only change. On the wall, there was a computer system complete with a camera, just like in every room.

The powers that be, namely the Komodian Administration, burned all the books and comics I had in a book burning ceremony which continued to take place every Monday. Even the stash I thought well hidden was no longer there. On the lower section of the computer that had been installed in my bedroom wall, I noticed a dispensary, which I quickly understood was where I would find my daily dose of psychological slavery.

I was going to have to get out of taking these pills one way or another until I could find some like-minded people to go undercover with. My next dose of Soma was scheduled for six hours from now; I was going to have to work fast and avoid detection.

My first thought was to turn on the TV, where I found out that Lord Komodo was going to be appearing on Earth in person the following day. The reason being that he wanted to celebrate humanity having been successfully assimilated into what he called "the proper way to live."

He appeared little different from the other Space Rangers, except he looked even more stoic.

I turned off the television, which was when my mother told me it was about time for the daily social skills class. These courses conditioned behaviors that would not take place as the Millennial 2084 virus caused people to walk around like zombies unless an authority, or a person not under the influence of the virus, gave them direction. Things like doing daily chores, getting information about the day's schedules, or instructing humans how to do their jobs took place daily. Humanity had become a people who were micromanaged. It was a miracle people could even breathe without being told to do so.

After it was over, I logged onto the internet, which no longer provided free information but outlined all the policies and procedures that had to be followed.

I eventually made my way outside, but there seemed to be no way of escaping the cameras and time was running out. Then the thought occurred to me- my family was under the influence of a drug that caused them to be susceptible to commands.

I began experimenting but had to do so discreetly because people behind the cameras were watching. I found when I asked my mother if she knew of anyone who had not taken the injection of the virus, that giving me that information was against the protocol that had been ingrained in her psyche through daily media conditioning. Plus, if she knew of anyone she would have already reported them to the proper authorities.

Not feeling that it was safe to go out alone, I convinced Samantha and my parents to go out for the rest of the day. When we went out, I recognized the sound of cicadas in the trees while we made our way down the long dirt road that Sam and I found ourselves faced with a situation that caused us to jump out of a moving car. When we arrived back home, I went back out and discovered that the cicada noises were actually coming from an alien species on humanoid insects who had made their home in their natural habitat of the trees.

I asked if any of them knew Muhammad, which I really felt was a fat chance, but wouldn't you know it- they gave me his last known whereabouts as anyone who asked a question to an infected person would receive an answer, which was why the Space Rangers wanted everyone to have the virus in their system. The body did not have any natural immunization properties for it, as the virus was part nanotechnology.

In the dead of night, after once again faking taking the medication, I got out of bed and began searching the internet and the phonebook for Muhammad, the taxicab driver. I narrowed down the search to a bakery who was owned by someone going by the name Muhammad Salvador. I figured that this would be my first option to check out as the rest did not seem to have as strong a likelihood. The research took several hours, so at three-thirty in the morning I quietly got dressed and took the keys to my father's Sedan.

On my way to the bakery, which I had a strong suspicion

had an upstairs apartment or would at least give me the opportunity to leave a note, the police pulled me over. The police wanted to know what I was doing out so late, as a mandatory curfew was in effect that kept anyone from being outside their home after ten o'clock.

"What seems to be the problem?" the police officer who pulled me over asked me as the bright flashing lights from his vehicle illuminated his face.

Pulling over right outside of my destination, I pointed to the building and answered the police honestly. "I was just going to see if my friend still lived here. I'm aware that it is past curfew but hoped that I could spend the night, or at least stay indoors, until sunrise."

The officer gave me a stern warning and said I had an honest face. Although he did run my driver's license and saw that I had no past or pending charges.

"In the future, you need to recognize that you cannot be out past curfew, but since you are on your way indoors, I will give you a warning. Please enjoy the rest of your night," the officer said with an obviously prefabricated protocol. He spoke into his radio, explaining the situation, and I could tell that his personality package lacked any sort of individuality. He probably did not think it was safe to have original ideas or even write anything down besides the things he wrote on tickets, like the warning he gave me that my parents still had to sign (as I was a former inmate who had recently returned to Earth).

The police officer drove off as I was about to walk up and knock on the door of the bakery. Yet, as I was about to exit my father's Sedan, I noticed a car discreetly pulling into the back alley. Instead of getting out and knocking on the door immediately, I attempted to find out who was in the Sonata. After some time, I recognized the car as the same one Sam and I had taken to my parents' house that night when the Space Rangers first invaded.

The person exiting the vehicle was wearing a gray coat and an enormous hat that concealed his face. Not wanting to startle the man, I pulled in beside him and flashed him with my bright headlights. The man approached the driver's side of the vehicle whence I saw his face, one that a keen observer could ascertain as artificial; it was indeed Muhammad.

"Is there something I can help you with, sir? You know it is awfully strange to be outside at this time of night, especially in an alley like this. I'm afraid I'll have to call the police if you don't leave...," warned Muhammad.

"Muhammad, it is me! Arnold Fitzgerald. Do you remember me and my boyfriend Samuel Yellowstone met you on the day of the invasion..."? I spoke, excited at seeing the alien.

A smile crept across my old friend's face. "Shh... yes, I remember you. I wondered what happened to you. Where is ol' Samuel anyway? It isn't every day that someone jumps out of the backseat of a moving car! What are you doing here?"

"It is a long story, well... Malcolm actually killed Samuel," I said as tears filled my eyes.

Muhammad expressed his condolences and mentioned how he wanted, "that bitch's ass above his fireplace."

"Anyway, I came to find you. See, I'm sure you have heard of the vaccination serum for the Millennial 2084 virus?" I asked.

"Yes, I'm quite familiar with it," confirmed Muhammad.

"Well, I've been given that and now the Gestapo is forcing me to take medication that counteracts it." Tears dropped from my face. "I just don't want to live that way. I would rather kill myself but my wife who I was forced to marry is pregnant, and I came searching for you because I hoped you would know what to do," I pleaded hopefully.

"Well, I suggest you best come on in with me and we will discuss what to do next," said Muhammad with a sigh of someone who felt both defeated and disgusted.

Muhammad led me across the road and into the bakery where a Middle Eastern man handed him a parcel enclosed in a white cloth before motioning us to go upstairs. Once we reached the top floor, I noticed how it was set up like a cramped apartment.

Taking off his social camouflage, Muhammad plopped down on an old, rugged couch. It was during that moment his aging became unmistakable to me. Despite his insect-like appearance, he hadn't shaved for several weeks and with deep pockets under his eyes- his facial expression was cemented with utter defeat.

"What is this place, Muhammad?" I inquired, not so much about what was clear, but more so interested in what he was thinking.

Since he was no longer using the Arabic disguise, his insect-like characteristics were visible, comprising of eyes that could see in countless directions. He scooted forward slowly on the couch and set both palms on his knees before speaking. Not knowing how emotionally involved he was, that question seemed to precipitate a psychological collapse of the mind.

"They've stolen everything from us! My spouse, my children… all my allies and relatives have turned against me because of that evil mind control serum!" declared a broken man with scarcely a leg left to stand on.

"Son, bring me the parcel Abdi handed us on the way up please," requested Muhammad.

I did as I was told, uncertain how I should feel and not knowing what to say in response to his anguish. We had all been affected by the invasion. Some just seemed more together than others.

He untied the white cloth; within the interior was a bottle of Cognac which he pointed out was unheard of to find anywhere on this world anymore, analogous to books composed by free-spirited thinkers.

He thrust open the bottle and consumed what had to have been half of it. Eyeing it shrewdly, he mentioned how the bottle was half full, leading me to speculate that despite the outright futility of the situation going on, there was some shimmer of hope.

I patiently waited for an explanation as the alcohol sunk in and replaced some of the suffering with numbness.

"Go ahead and glance around... I'm sorry I don't seem to recall your..."

"Arnold, sir, Arnold Fitzgerald. We clashed in your taxi when the Space Rangers first appeared," I tore in before he concluded his sentence.

"Yes, I remember that night well. It was the same night Malcolm began spreading the virus and turning human civilization into despotism! I was fortuitous to have not been captured by the Gestapo! In fact, a few days after I drove my darn car off the bridge into the creek I dug it out and repaired the entire thing from the ground up. But I didn't succeed alone..." Muhammad reminisced.

"Who has been helping you?" I inquired, hopeful for a resistance force.

Muhammad's eyes flickered. "It is rare that anyone asks a question like that anymore- we are too caught up in controversy and staying out of mind's eye... the eye of the totalitarian reign of Lord Komodo. The world has become leery of anyone asking questions- many of us who have never been seen or heard of again!" scorned Muhammad.

Muhammad squeezed the bottle tight and chugged the rest of the Cognac before planting his head between his insectoid limbs.

"Go look around son and things will start making sense directly," declared a man who had just about taken his last breath many times as it pertained to giving up on being part of the intransigent rebellion.

Apart from the empty bottles of Cognac that were piling up, probably having been delivered by his friends that I still did not know about, there was a modest kitchen/living area, a bath directly across the entrance to the hallway, and two cramped bedrooms, one of which was unoccupied. There wasn't much in the decoration department.

"You'll be living in this room Arnold- but you'll have to sleep on the couch in the living room until we can muster up a way or some money to get ahold of a mattress," declared Muhammad, who had inched up behind me. "What do you think- we might even take the couch cushions off and make you a little nest in here if you'd be more comfortable?"

Muhammad stepped into the room of the apartment, which I was increasingly realizing was discreet, not consisting on any windows, and almost indiscernible from the street below. The room had little more than some worn out carpet and a rubbish bin that was full of Cognac bottles.

Suddenly I noticed the door to the closet was slightly ajar by only a hair. I peeped inside the dimly lit room and noticed a wardrobe that comprised disguises of all types- obviously Muhammad was not the only one to take part in the ritual of hiding his genuine identity.

"What's in here?" I asked curiously with the vague reluctance stemming from my desire for Samuel to still be alive and with me at that moment. He would've been happy for this reunion.

"We have had many young up-and-comers who had to learn rapidly that asking questions isn't a safe idea in this time and place. You simply can't just go around asking questions or sharing things about yourself without being interrogated. And once you are interrogated, unless they detect an unyielding sense of loyalty, the situation will be turned around on you and will amount to more trouble than you'd bet your britches on.

"We just live in the type of place where every detail concerning how social interactions should take place is controlled and heavily monitored. But take a gander at the closet and I'm sure you'll be surprised at what you find," suggested Muhammad.

Opening the door to the closet, it reached me with the odor of grease and lead. With what must have been a million dollars' worth of weapons, technology, and masks used for disguises- the first thing that caught my eye were the sniper rifles sitting all across both sides of the closet.

"Aren't you worried about someone finding out about this stuff, Muhammad?" I asked, nervous and bewildered.

"Every day, Arnold, every darn day."

"What's it all for? I mean..." I sputtered, "I understand it is being used in the fight against the Space Rangers... right?" I sounded a bit like an interrogator.

"Come on and get some dinner Abdi left for us. It is in the bag you brought up. I will reveal our plans in the morning." I wasn't pleased my question was left unanswered but figured morning would come soon enough. It had been a long enough day.   Becoming mindful of how ravenous I was, we went into the kitchen and ate what I came to know as a proper meal comprising bread, dried meat, and wine. When we finished, Muhammad showed me how to clean up and put away the dishes.

"I get little sleep these days, Arnold. Even when I lay down, my dreams are filled with the vile goings-on of the ruthless and psychotic chain of command of this planet. The plots and conspiracies of Lord Komodo's regime keep me up at night, and to be honest, I've slaughtered enough of his soldiers to understand why I am frightened for my life."

He studied at me with an expression so serious I almost wet my trousers.

"Take some rest my boy- it may be the last decent night sleep you'll ever have… but let's hope not," sighed Muhammad as he got up from the couch and somberly walked into the second bedroom, I had not yet had the chance to snoop into.

I contemplated how it may have been a better idea to have continued to live with my parents and accepted the pill that would regulate how I thought. Subsequently, I grabbed the blanket hanging over the worn-out pink couch and closed my eyes for what seemed like minutes before I was awakened by a series of footsteps approaching up the stairs.

x

I opened my eyes for the first time that day. A radio was playing static but was soon tuned, and I attended my mind to the sounds of a newscaster, which piqued my attention.

"Today marks a historical milestone in Earth's cosmic history," announced an amiable but clearly non-human voice. "For the first time, Lord Komodo himself will present 'A Celebration for Human Appreciation'. His Majesty himself will arrive in just a few hours to show his recognition of mankind choosing to receive his authority in leadership and presence as their deity," reported the newscaster with great hype.

The transmission cut off abruptly, and I began overhearing mumbled voices from Muhammad's area.

I shoved the blanket off and got out of the bed I had formed on the couch. Looking around the apartment and noticing things I hadn't the night before, I scampered around in my underwear until I located my jeans. With my slightly hairy chest exposed, I made my way into the bathroom where I relieved myself. Not knowing what I was going to be part of, I took a shower and tried to wrap my head around everything that had happened since Sam had died. I realized, now that I could think for myself once again, that I had more questions than answers about my current predicament.

Once I finished putting on my clothes, I used Muhammad's bathroom supplies (which were in abundance owing to his habit of concealing himself) to brush my hair and straighten up the dirty clothes I was wearing. I would have to ask my host how to go about finding a toothbrush and deodorant later that day, if at all feasible.

Cleaning up after myself and dangling my wet towel on the rack to dry, I fully turned my awareness back to the scene going on in the apartment. Leaving the bathroom, the solemn face of Muhammad abruptly greeted me.

"In most instances, we would train you in our standard operating strategies and keep you hidden, but today, out of a need for a fourth man, we've agreed to include you in our plans. We've determined to make do with what we have to work with," declared my host.

I was determined to do anything it took, including sacrificing my life, in order for humanity to reclaim its right to experience psychological freedom. Looking Muhammad dead in the eyes and with total confidence, I replied, "What's the plan?"

CHAPTER 13

The next several minutes comprised of being introduced to Muhammad's squad. There was Abdi, who I recognized from being at the bakery below the residence we were presently staying in. Then we had, to my astonishment, a Space Ranger who we called Venessa, an erstwhile staff member of Malcolm's who had been abducted by Muhammad and Abdi.

The reason for this was because Muhammad had a plan to fight back, albeit something that would inevitably only be petty; but he wanted to piss off what he considered irrational authority just for the sake of making a stance. Finally, there was Zeke, who was an elegant and muscular human. After we had been introduced, I found out he was from a modest municipality in Illinois.

There was an immediate connection between Zeke and me, which was ratified by him throwing me a wink, followed by a gigantic grin. The five of us made our way into the rear room as intended by the team leader, Muhammad.

"The plan is straightforward but oh-so-sophisticated," declared Muhammad, who began securing weapons onto his bulletproof vest, which encompassed a multitude of compartments.

Feeling that I was the focus of awareness as all their eyes concentrated on me, I summoned up the audacity to ask the most obvious question, "Are we going to assassinate Lord Komodo?"

Muhammad's grave eyes clashed with mine as he acknowledged with, "Komodo is a murdering psychopath who has enslaved dozens of planets in this arm of the Milky Way. Saying that we were going to assassinate him would do him homage, as only people who have lived righteously can be assassinated. No Arnold, we are going to kill a dictator."

The company analyzed my feedback and was relieved to find out that I would not be a coward or "pussy out." But suddenly, suspicions made the best of me as I stepped towards Muhammad in disbelief.

"You can't honestly think that you can kill a well-protected dictator with a few simple disguises, some sniper rifles, and this small team, do you?" I examined it too obnoxiously.

x

Around the time that the conference was taking place, we stood witness in front of the television to Lord Komodo's ship touching down at a secure location within the foreign nation's capital. Hundreds of surveillance personnel and loaded vehicles equipped with advanced technology swarmed the district all the way to the peripheries. Every window of every home or place of business within fifty miles of where the tyrant would present his speech was heavily supervised.

Extra quantities of Millennial 2084 were being distributed via gas and through the water all over the globe. Many of those identified to be in hiding during that time, comprising every conscientious objector that could be detected and located, were also given heavy doses of this virus, which abolished the free will and individuality of consciousness.

At this same moment, many of the policies that had been pending were confirmed with approval because of the nervousness and impending feelings of doom from those continuing to resist despite the effects of the remedy. It was a time where thinking was not permitted due to the fact that any kind of unauthorized contemplation was not allowed. Policies that gave the Space Rangers what they wanted because if Komodo did not see that humans were cooperative, there was no telling what wrath he would lay waste to us with.

Komodo stepped out of the space vessel like a king. The world hailed him with thundering applause and unconditional reverence.

"Okay Arnold, it is time for you to understand what I've been hiding in my room," announced Muhammad.

I trotted behind Zeke and, despite the enormity of the situation, could not help but look over his well-toned body as he strode into the room with masculine warmth.

Inside the room, a green screen hung from the wall. In front of it were cameras, and all over the room was high-tech recording equipment. A wave of uneasiness swept from the back of my head down to the seat of my spine, nearly making me shiver.

I twisted around to Muhammad instinctively and remarked, "What could we possibly do that wouldn't cause us to get captured?"

"Venessa, maybe you can explain this phase of the plan to Arnold?" requested Muhammad.

Muhammed stepped aside and gestured to Venessa to tell me about the plan that I felt I would promptly be a part of. Venessa stepped closer to me in a fashion somewhat similar to every member of her species I have faced- patronizing and proud.

"Listen Arnold, our plot is to set up a scene, to make it look like something it is not... and now that we have you, the stakes have gone up even higher," she said with a derisive expression.

What happened next surprised me, or rather seized me off guard. My first impression was that things between Venessa and I were going well, especially since we had just been introduced.

But that impression transformed into something uglier when she spat in my face.

"Just because we're working together does not mean we're friends!" Venessa sputtered furiously.

In a state of shock, I cleaned the saliva from my face and looked shyly at Zeke. Evidently, there was more going on between this group of people than first occurred to me. Before I could express how confused I was, Muhammed pushed a button on his watch, which delivered waves of electricity searing through Venessa's nerves via a necklace ingeniously camouflaged as pearls.

"Listen scumbag, I don't care what gender you are- but as long as you are my captive, all you are is Space Ranger scum!" shouted Muhammad.

Zeke trotted forward and punched Venessa in the abdomen, causing her to double over slightly.

"The two of you need to go retrieve a pistol from the back closet. This could get messy," sighed Muhammad.

x

Zeke and I went into the closet in the back room. I shut the door behind me as he was the first to enter.

"Hey fella, what was that all about? I expect I have the right to some answers!" I announced anxiously, still exacerbated by the episode I had just witnessed.

Zeke crouched over and began rummaging through a box for the pistol. His perfectly shaped muscular buttocks looked dazzling in the baggy jeans he was wearing. Though because I was still in a fit of annoyance I ignored such trivialities.

Zeke found two handguns and offered one to me.

"What am I supposed to do with this?" I demanded, knowing I had never even shot a gun in my life. Zeke instructed me how to use the weapon, including how to load, unload, and cock the pistol and carefully showed how to use the safety features multiple times before requiring me to model what he had just taught. He fastened a holster onto my name brand pants, which made my butt look awesome, and declared that I would need to have something to protect myself with or possibly even save him with.

"Can you at least inform me what my job is going to be during this stage of the plan?" I responded in a high-pitched tone that arose out of excitement and anxiousness.

Zeke placed one finger over my lips, which elicited a sensational response.

"Arnold, the entire plan is doomed to fail and get us all captured. I'm not even totally sure what the plan is. I'm just following what Muhammad says, including capturing Venessa. We've been sheltering her in my parents' basement for about a year now and everyone seems to have forgotten about her; though there were heavy-duty searches across Washington, D.C. when the awareness of her absence first arose. He helped me get off medication and remain undetected in society. Yeah, he's constantly calling me a useless, dimwitted idiot. I'm not sure what I would do without him. Whatever the plan is, I'm reasonably sure it is risky and not fully thought out."

Zeke ran his finger down my chest and settled it on the zipper of my pants. He kissed me smoothly on the lips seductively and said, "Once you have lived outside the mainstream views- the world doesn't look the same. I'm just along for the ride."

After that, the two of us found ourselves conscious of our choice to strip each other completely. At first, I turned him down because I was more concerned about the mission to save humanity from the evils of despotism, which had at this point been able to achieve seizing control of our free will. Free will, which I defined as losing the ability to ask questions for ourselves and being unable to engage in self-directed behaviors not assigned by a superior. I felt that if there was a way to debase the authority of the Space Rangers and, in doing so, save humanity from the totalitarian dictatorship that continued to rise in prominence, I would help with it. And if accomplishing that goal means I have to lie, cheat, and steal- I would do that too. I was already a fugitive once more.

Zeke mentioned we should live every day as if it were our last. He sounded entirely unafraid of danger, lacked any sort of insecurity like he was ready to march full speed into a psychological plot that, as he suggested and was becoming more conspicuous to me by the minute, was doomed to fail. So, as Zeke continued to kiss me in an alluring fashion, which was not unwanted, I decided the well-being of humanity could wait for just a few more minutes because hell, even a potential martyr (as I was prepared to risk my life to save humanity) needs to have fun sometimes.

This determination was made while Zeke's kisses progressed further down towards my happy trail. At that point, I could not resist unbuttoning his pants, and in a matter of seconds, the two of us were altogether in the buff. While this was taking place, I was reminded of the same experience that took place with my previous boyfriend, Samuel.

I pushed the memories of Sam's blood dripping from my hands and face as his deceased carcass was ripped away from me by her guards, and I stood upright with my hands fastened to one shelf. I did this primarily because that was not how I wanted to remember Sam; I wanted to remember him as the boy I had met in college who could play my heart like the strings on a guitar. For the fact of the matter is, I wouldn't be alive today were it not for Sam's courage.

x

Moments after what can solely be described as a firework show, once the grand finale had taken place, Muhammad's robust voice was heard calling our names from the room with the green screen.

We hastily dressed and aided each other in looking presentable once again.

"Sorry boss- we're on our way," called a grinning Zeke.

Going back into the front bedroom, we experienced an uncanny cognitive reality. Given how we'd just experienced such profound pleasure and were eminently happy afterward, visually interpreting the grim and angry physiognomy of someone who had lost everything- including his wife and children to these Space Rangers- the two of us immediately became immersed in the sobering experience of dread and culpability.

"Now, I hope you realize how entirely vain it is to continue living under the guise of despotism, through which we are merely pretending to be 'thoughtless' organisms who are subordinate to an immoral, tyrannical regime. This totalitarian dictatorship's only desire is for us to be expressionless beings that worship the very feet of their narcissistic dictator. Who, if you haven't noticed, is not actually God- we must progress to the later phase of the plan!"

Out of rage for the entire situation, Muhammad struck Venessa with his ring finger, leaving behind a gash across her face. Enraged, she knew there was nothing she could do without further retribution.

Then from the living room space that was likewise a kitchen, we heard a voice emanate an announcement.

"We would now like to ask for perfect silence as our eternal god Komodo takes the stage on this day to celebrate our acceptance to serve under his supreme administration," said the scripted voice of a human female.

The mindless woman proceeded, "May his words of wisdom be adhered to as an edict. Keep in mind that we should all be wary that anybody who disobeys risks utter repudiation, ignominy and austere ostracization from our Galactic Union[16]. We bear witness to the fact that those of us who do not submit and cooperate daily will unquestionably be reproached and bemoan their contumacious conduct."

The audience sat there emotionless and looked to any intelligent person like the most idiotic people to have ever lived, almost robotic waiting to be programmed. With the announcement, the crowd's expression changed to plaster smiles on their faces, which were put there on purpose by the authorities of their lives.

It became undeniable that Muhammad not only hated the man, but that he mocked superiority. Years afterward, he would describe how easy it was to exploit and poke fun at people whose cognitive dispositions viewed themselves as superior. He would remark how someone can only be insubordinate if they are indeed a subordinate to begin with, that being subordinate only insinuates that the ego was submissive, for one does not need to be subordinate to function in society.

In fact, Muhammad and I observed years later, nearly a decade after this story concluded, that the Millennial 2084 virus acted on the brain to make organisms submissive. It can well be understood from this that submissive behavior was what lead to the de-evolution of the Plecostomus people.

From this, Muhammad arrived at the verdict that submissiveness was the key factor that was most pernicious to the repudiation of free will. The love of learning was what most heightened a person's ability to verbalize the mental extension of intellectual horizons via the enunciation of freedom that bears with it the apex of cognitive experience, that being of independent volition and autonomy from the oppression of liberty by authority or else wise one's own rivaled peer group.

x

 For all the hype and commotion about the famous Komodo visiting Planet Earth for the first time, his presence was fairly humdrum. He presented much like every other Space Ranger, except he had a tail, which I recently learned every member of his species was born with. Interestingly enough, the entire population of Space Ranger had their tails removed at birth. Those that did not were viewed as atheistic, and this was a way of keeping track of the political divide between the different ideologies.

 Yet, the incontestable fact of the matter, regardless of his display of personality, was that his psychological prowess was unrivaled. Suggesting that we contend with this father of demigods was not only absurd, but even speaking about it was a serious infraction.

 Our ragtag group comprising of Muhammad, Abdi, Zeke, myself, and one hostage waited to discover how this being who enslaved entire civilizations would begin his speech- yet it was not an entire surprise as many of his speeches were available over the strictly regulated Web, which underwent incredible technological upgrades via introducing "Space Ranger" technology [NBA: I used quotations because truth be told, Space Rangers never invented very much during their recorded history but used the inventions of other species.]. Technology of which the Council of Planets was wary of allocating to human beings.

 Yet, now that the Space Rangers had preempted the authority of the council, human beings now had the very means of producing technology with the collective intelligence of all the known species in the galaxy. Technology that is only surpassed by the machinery of The Ancients, who are said to navigate to other galaxies and whose minds possess cognitive strengths that Komodo only claims to have in check.

In fact, during his pursuit to capture and enslave one of The Ancient's species, he intended to outmaneuver them and claim ownership of their technology. This was the primary motive in positing the status and portraying the intellectual prestige that he did; though the evils of despotism became apparent through the years of his reign, his strategy was indeed admirable.

x

Human beings were now part of the intergalactic culture- some would claim the Council of Planets, if they could be said to remain, permitted Homo Sapiens to be controlled by the Millennial 2084 virus. While simultaneously, the Space Rangers also now had oversight of the council, though many of the senators had retreated- at least those who had not been apprehended and made captives. Even if senators could keep their position on the council, they had no genuine power or say in anything the way Komodo manipulated things.

The cameras concentrated on Lord Komodo and transmitted a mandatory viewing all around the spherical globe.

This person who was much feared and reported to be the czar of the Milky Way Galaxy was afforded a microphone as he strode onto the stage in Beijing, China where folks from every area of the world including London, Pairs, Rome, Cozumel, Honduras, Kingston, Santiago, Los Angeles, Kabul, Stockholm, Oslo, Helsinki, Havana, Athens, Zimbabwe and elsewhere were instructed to observe reverently.

The Komodo Administration made extensive endeavors to present the video recording, or at least the audio, to technologically challenged sections of the spherical globe. This speech was copied and to be played daily throughout the realm henceforth and in non-human territories, much like the political propaganda I had seen from other worlds.

What we predicted at first was for His Noble Majesty to deliver a tremendous hurrah. Yet, to the frightened surprise of the world, Komodo began his address in an unobtrusive and effortless way that rapidly intensified and beguiled the awareness of the world state.

Seeming to have not taken part in any sort of cognitive transformation from the time he sauntered onto the stage and the moment where he lifted his microphone, Komodo began:

"Subordinates of my authority, I have appeared here now to witness firsthand your species' submission to my rule. Being cognizant of the psychological underpinnings of any matter of social condition has not only become redundant because of my engagement in every instance, but I also prohibited you from having a heightened grasp of awareness!

"My authority reigns over any social condition, and you will work collectively for my approval and nothing more! You may write, you may THINK, and you may discuss, but you will NOT have the autonomy to do so as you please- this I answer with the utmost severity which I sustain will ultimately amount in your disposal; but before that arises, I have in place the means to make life very difficult for you. And if my personal involvement were to become necessary, I assure you that misery has not yet entered your vocabulary.

"My presence here on Earth exists, and it exists so prominently. Though I may have other matters to attend to, I assure you, news of your disobedience will reach me quickly!"

x

As Komodo continued speaking, our party, managed by Muhammad, hurriedly activated our machinery, which had been perfectly refined by Abdi. Whilst this was happening, Venessa was strategically placed in front of the green screen.

Muhammad handed her the manuscript and Zeke held

up five fingers, counting down to zero. Venessa appeared nonplussed for seconds because of the helplessness of her situation. Then, as clearly as the sun does rise, Venessa's image appeared on the left side of the screen while feed from Komodo appeared on the right- on every gadget in the world. Being seen by billions of people, an audience vaster than any recorded in Earth's history, Komodo was visibly astonished by the ability and gall of whoever was applying this tactic against him.

CHAPTER 14

Several moments of being dumbfounded occurred during which a priceless expression was broadcasted over the television satellites. Whilst this took place, Venessa's mind traveled through the deepest catacombs of thought ever to have taken place in her life. Through sheer desperation, Venessa soon processed a secret plot, unbeknownst to anyone else. Seizing the opportunity to press forward and appear to our party as if she was simply following our directions, she gathered her wits and progressed in reading from the script.

Venessa began following her role in perfect synchrony and with such precision that it was eerie. Muhammad's ego inflated exponentially, though the entire time his captive had constructed a scheme that could have only been discovered in the most desperate of social positions- she broke from the chain of command. Her tone and demeanor reflected the script so exquisitely that it could be said she was living on the same cognitive level as the best of men in the worst of times. It should also be said that her ultimate plan was that Komodo would understand her desperate situation.

"The name I go by since splitting from the chain of command is Venessa, but you may call me V," she hesitated long enough for Komodo to recognize he had little choice but to address this person who was once his inferior subservient.

Tense and in a nervous alacrity because of falling to the perception of the veracity of who she was tête-à-tête with, Venessa amassed a depth of cognitive status she never suspected was possible. She verbalized from the script without breaking character and resonated like the extraordinary person whom Muhammad had understood she could be while composing the dialogue. She appeared as an icon of cognitive emancipation who had conquered a life destitute of love and who had overcome the psychological oppression of her ancestors. The script read as follows,

"Societies of the Milky Way and Lord Komodo. We have intercepted your broadcast in order to assert that this autocracy will not continue!"

Lord Komodo appeared flabbergasted as he and Venessa made eye contact over the screen. In fact, being that the reverence she owed Komodo was altogether predicated on the trepidation of psychological retaliation, this was not unlike something Venessa would have relished to have done in her wildest dreams; though simultaneously, the oath she had pledged to Komodo since childhood was too vigorous for her to surrender completely to her dream of perspicacious liberation.

Venessa perpetuated with an ease of transition. "At this moment, I would relish calling for avail from anyone who is tuning in to this transmission. Anyone who can be of any aid, please do so now! We will not allow this aggression to stand, and we are certain that others exist who are pugnacious enough to stand beside us! The psychological oppression you have subjected countless planets to is over once and for all. Surrender now or face the consequences!" She read as if she had inscribed it.

As Zeke and I were operating the cameras, we overheard what sounded like a herd of locus hovering over the house. I squinted out the blinds in Muhammad's room, the only room with windows, and observed what had to be at least one hundred military officers circumventing the house we were in, including dozens of helicopters swarming above.

This is what Venessa had expected all along. She had seen

firsthand the strength of mind and military perspicuity of Komodo. Venessa knew that any strike against him in the slightest was not simply futile, but was also certain to get you killed.

Yet the plight wasn't the fact that she knew Komodo's security would pinpoint their location in a matter of minutes- it was what would transpire to her afterward. Either way, she looked at it. She was logically certain she would not outlive the night, but Komodo's lifelong promise to his subordinates to keep them safe was ever present in her hopeful mind.

Receiving a radio transmission from the security personnel outside the bakery, Komodo stood up from the chair that had been brought to him and declared, "Exit the bakery with your hands up and preserve the little regard I still have for you! Whoever you are, you've taken one of my own as a hostage, and I would very much like for this to culminate as a rescue and not as a martyrdom!

"If you honestly believe you could commit this attack against me and that I would not be qualified to handle the situation and make an example out of you, then you are seriously mistaken! In fact, a declaration of belligerence at this level is not only an act of confrontation, but it makes you more insane than you could have ever possibly imagined! If this showdown is to take place, so be it!" declared Komodo.

"Continue reading the script, Venessa," ordered Muhammad. But this time, he walked in front of the camera and held a pistol to his victims' cranium.

Venessa wept fearfully and the primary audience Komodo had come to Earth to deliver this address to expressions changed from idiotic smiles to that of those who were moved emotionally by her tears. Even though they had no awareness of what was actually going on, they still held the captive Space Ranger in an authoritative position and reacted to her lead.

The last part of the script read, "Tell the truth." This was a directive for Venessa to tell the world exactly what she had learned through being a captive over the last year and what it meant to her to be in the position that she was today.

Venessa got her weeping under control and, through her desperation, spoke the following words to anyone listening in the galaxy. "I agree with my captors. Turning people into mindless subordinates of an irrational authority is not right…"

Komodo was becoming more agitated by the second. At the same time, he was impressed by his subordinate having said something which did not get her killed in that instant. Yet, he was dissonant with this feeling, though, because he felt that staying alive for a few more minutes was not worth sacrificing a lifelong faithfulness to his administration; while also considering the fact that she must have undergone intense brainwashing over the year she was kidnapped. Given his god-like prominence, he felt he understood how his followers felt better than anyone, which was substantiated because he handled how she was educated as a child and that the same Reperoritian blood ran through her veins.

x

Now you must, for want of understanding, allow me to tell you how Komodo gained the political power he did until this point. It really isn't hard to understand, frankly. Though eventually he used other people to work his way to the top, which psychologists of Earth during the aftermath of these significant events in history later described as the developmental process of becoming a sociopath, in reality, this wasn't accurate.

Lord Komodo originally only wanted to see his family and community rise out of poverty- even though he was taught poverty was the nature of peace and was a virtue. Having the opinion that he would be the one to implement changes in society, his rise to power was not one of violence but was simply a matter of chance. When the time to meet The Ancients would come, they knew his political rise to power was born from the desire to abolish the old way of thinking on his planet to one where his people could be sustained.

As a child, Komodo was one of the few from the planet Reperoritas to keep their tail. Almost all children at the time of birth had their tails removed except those who spiritual leaders selected to become future religious leaders. This matter was not taken lightly, as the Reperoritian believed that raising a child to have reverence for a universal deity would instill in them a character that would qualify them as future leaders. His childhood was filled with challenges that tested his faith in himself and his spirituality. Their planet based its organization on the spiritual enlightenment that took centuries to learn.

His peers within the monasteries he devoted his life to living in during his childhood spurned him for having been selected from an impoverished family. When the chiefs recognized this, they further selected him for opportunities the other children did not have. The leaders did this because they understood that a life of hardship helped to develop character, and they wanted to make sure they were not being biased in their opinions. When they discovered he continued to give praises and help the less fortunate, despite his higher position, he was assigned the greatest title of schooling and spiritual training that their esteem could offer.

Then, like a fallen angel, Komodo broke away from the religion he was brought up with in order to claim that he had received enlightenment surpassing what he was taught to believe during his spiritual education. He would have never even thought about breaking away from the chain of command were it not because his core ideals were vehemently shaken when he saw how poverty-stricken his world was during trips outside the monasteries.

Like the monks who want to make changes on Earth, Komodo wanted to solve the social conflicts his people were facing.

Issues that the spiritual leaders saw as a way of keeping the planet out of the affairs of other planets and keeping peace on Reperoritas. Komodo instead saw this as a way for them to maintain control.

In his writings, he portrayed himself as someone who would expose the deceitfulness of the spiritual leaders. Yet Komodo inwardly understood that he was behaving out of a desire to compensate from being rejected. Deciding to start his own doctrine, he published what he had written about the degeneracy of the spiritual chiefs and how the world needed a political leader who could lead his people into a new era.

After a century of teaching the enlightenment he claimed to have gathered through an incorporeal awakening of the mind, he had accumulated a following. After that, he was considered a threat to the peace and the spiritual leaders cross-examined him during a judicial hearing. Of course, it was not a crime to think differently on his planet, but Komodo was causing a great deal of uncertainty within the monasteries, which was why he was expelled.

The chiefs within the monasteries said his expulsion was warranted in that he was not keeping the peace. He was placed in a prison for the ideologically deviant population, whence he created schemes and plots to liberate his world from political oppression; again, what he thought was the right thing to do. Eventually, the people of Reperoritas demanded to hear his voice, and when it was heard by the general population, he was exonerated and accepted back into society. They even allowed him to keep his tail which was to be cut off in prison.

It wasn't until he began educating people within the general population that he worked his way up to a political elite. His experience in being expelled from the monasteries gained him fame, and his outspoken nature about societal issues such as the problem of political correctness gained him a seat in a leadership position that set him up to run for president.

After he ran a tough campaign whereby he claimed that becoming part of the galactic community would be good for the planet (while his opponent was of the opposite nature), the votes were cast and Komodo was elected as president. Whence he became part of the Milky Way Council of Planetary Peace.

As a senator for the council, Komodo was recognized as coming from a planet that was peaceful, as it had had no intentional bloodshed in centuries because of the spiritual nature of its people. After being given the offer, he allowed the habitable planets in his solar system to become The System of Correction, whereby people who broke the peace would be sentenced to stay and receive treatment before they could reenter society.

This line of work for the Reperoritians became profitable and his people no longer lived in poverty, which was what Komodo wanted to accomplish all along. Yet, he had so much trouble meeting the quotas and designing effective treatments that would enable criminals to reintegrate into society that he pushed for the legalization of the use of the Millennial 2084 virus, which eradicated the central nervous system's ability to act on its own free will.

Having the most experience in dealing with matters concerning war crimes and people who were bent on creating problems between planets, the council took deep consideration in Komodo's plea to legalize Millennial 2084. And so, after a capricious vote, plans to use the virus to cure the criminally inclined included investing more money into The System of Correction. Eventually, the council allowed Reperoritas to rename itself after Komodo, who begrudgingly announced that he had received further enlightenment from the gods and that his people would now refer to him as Lord Komodo.

Keeping in mind that the System of Correction was established 150 years prior to the discovery of Millennial 2084; it wasn't until around that same time that the council became aware that humanity was about to discover space travel. Prior to this, decades went by that the Space Rangers directed the affairs of the treatment facilities (for those who could not function without causing a disturbance). These facilities took up most of the space on each of the planets besides Reperoritas (Komodo's home planet).

Reperoritas remained a planet that only natives could visit but what is known is the political debates that took place regarding the activities on the other planets in their solar system (known as the System of Correction). Even with his busy schedule regulating the affairs his job description allotted, Komodo performed research that showed the existence of life beyond the Orion Arm. It was during this historical event that he discovered new information about a race who were known only as The Ancients.

After that, Komodo searched every habitable planet, and some uninhabitable, for information concerning this race, and finally the council allowed him to visit Planet Earth because of their technological achievements, but only under the premise that he infected humanity with the Millennial 2084 virus.

It was an easy call by the Council of Planets to use the Millennial 2084 virus on Earth, who saw humanity's potential to wage war with other planets as they had their own neighboring nations. Which worked out well for Komodo, who was still looking for information about The Ancients.

Before Earth was invaded, Komodo was successful in finding a constellation chart, but from what constellation, he did not know. Malcolm was placed in charge of deciphering the map, but wasn't successful either. Years later, after King Thaddeus had been captured and used his telepathy to control Jamie, who had been infected with Millennial 2084 so that he could escape her clutches, that he took the star chart off of Malcolm's ship (depicting foreign constellations) with him.

Lord Komodo found out that Thaddeus's scientist Ramos Destin Uphanivan unlocked the key to his puzzle after he captured and questioned a council member who had attended the meeting in which The Ancients brought the vaccination to Earth. This did not take place until a great deal after my boyfriend Samuel Yellowstone had been killed by Malcolm's guards, and that is why Komodo began testing humans for antibodies.

The Reperoritian had allowed his obsession with finding The Ancients to consume him because, by that time, he received a continuance of his presidency. By having the aim of finding The Ancients and the location of their planet, Komodo had a direction to go in that fit in with the Council of Planets' mission statement of establishing peace in the Orion Arm of the Milky Way.

The Ancients, once they were found, could share their technology with Komodo, who would use it to end wars and establish peace... if there were such a thing. For this reason, he knew that the sustainability of The System of Correction would need an alternative solution or else the posterity of the people of his home planet Reperoritas was once again in jeopardy.

The aspect that there was a technology that could be used as a means for good in helping maintain peace came to Komodo as a viable option. It is for this reason he started his pursuit to locate The Ancient's because it was a positive direction to go in, while continuing to do the same old thing- using this debilitaing virus to maintain peace- was not sustainable. That there were other options gave Komodo hope, yet that is what so many of the people who fought the use of the virus did not understand. Komodo had expressed his desire to locate The Ancients, but nobody on the council believed it was possible or even rational.

Lord Komodo was not a perfect person, but as someone who erred, his imperfections made him a person. The amount of power got to his head, and becoming a dictator was likely not something he did not want. Who would? He told himself that the council put him in charge of keeping organization, but when the council would not help him locate The Ancients, he broke away from the regimented order of their bureaucratic protocols. They, like the spiritual leaders from before, had failed.

Of course, Komodo never actually created armies, though rumors of him doing so occurred. The planets the virus was used on were run similarly to Earth. The council technically broke apart into the faction those who were pro-virus and those who were anti-virus. This was when Komodo realized he could use the virus to his advantage, due to his line of work.

Allowing his people to bring the sentient life-forms of Polunin, where Thaddeus was king, to the brink of extinction was done without his approval. Still, Komodo eventually greedily ransacked the planet, hoping to get ahold of the technology the scientist Ramos Destin Uphanivan used.

Having not captured the eminent scientist was what Komodo confessed later that he was ashamed of. This was because there was no telling what genius inventions Ramos could have developed, especially if the two of them worked together. It was a great crime against sentient life to have murdered a mind with that ferocious of intelligence; albeit it was not Komodo's fault he was killed.

Whether real evil exists in this story has nothing to do with the people who were elected as leaders. Rather, it was the consequences of having good intentions coupled with poor decisions. I contend though, similar to myself, that just because someone or a body of people make a mistake- they are still good people. The people who were trusted to place others in leadership positions had high standards, and they did the right thing by wanting to have ethically minded people in charge.

At the same time, the council's decision to sponsor the System of Correction was never done with ill intentions. As the facilities located on those planets with harsh weather conditions continued to grow, it began to become apparent that the whole idea wasn't, in fact, a good idea. So, when the Armodafians discovered the pathogen built with nanotechnology and began experimenting with it, it soon became advertised. The council was largely misguided in purchasing the formula to replicate the virus to begin with, because it wasn't until much later that the greedy Armodafians came forward with the information about de-evolution. De-evolution which they had witnessed when they discovered the virus within the bodies of the Plecostomus people and comparing them to fossil remains of their ancestors.

Komodo urged the council and indeed did place great pieces on the table to influence the vote in his favor. Yet again though, this was so that the System of Correction- consisting of a few planets and moons that had been terraformed in his home solar system- would continue generating the profit needed to advance the economy of his own society. Not only that, but he and the majority of the council did not know what to do with the inmates who were being reformed at his facilities.

The politics over the Millennial 2084 virus were very misunderstood, especially by the council members themselves. What caused the most apprehension was the fact that most of the council members never anticipated there to be any other option that could replace the temporary solution (which was why it was unofficially declared as a permanent solution). Moreover, once an alternative direction could be set into motion, not all the council members were convinced that giving up on their original decision would be the logical course of action.

CHAPTER 15

I will tangentially express about the upbringing of Komodo and the tangent about why he wasn't a hate-filled person. What is thought to have caused the opinion of Komodo being twisted and evil was partly due to the progression of events-those taking place since the discovery of the nanotechnology pathogen and the council voting on whether to use it or not occurring too quickly in succession. The other half of the equation was how Komodo, through the process of rising through the hierarchy of leadership, acquired his own administration separate from that of the Orion Arm Council of Peace.

Komodo's administration, which consisted of Space Rangers that the council had originally hired to operate the System of Correction, began to make their own decisions about how the offenders should be educated. Even though the Space Rangers were paid to come up with ways of keeping the society of mind slaves organized, the council was responsible for oversight-oversight that was often ignored by the Komodian Administration. It was overlooked in how the Space Rangers created a regiment for those thought to be a threat to the peace between and amongst planets that gave the illusionary cognitive perception of Komodo having become the person who had the most power.

The fact that the people who raised Komodo rejected him after they saw statues of him being placed in ways that made him look like he was above all the things they held holy did not help matters. He began to side with the decision making of people he put in charge because they had power to get things done. Inwardly Komodo felt like he was in a position that he could never escape from. But as he saw the quality of life on his planet increase as wealth began to grow, he cast aside his moral uncertainty over the well-being of people on other planets. This was because he felt it was his responsibility to take care of his people first.

The task to find technology that would alleviate the current behavioral solution (as it pertains to Millennial 2084) was beginning to feel impossible, which in turn caused hopelessness. It was rumored that The Ancients had technology that would create new opportunities. Finding this technology is what kept Komodo keeping up with appearances. He did a great deal of negotiating with people in the council and many official policies and procedures were enacted. President Vevo's position began to shrink as Komodo's agenda began to take on more and more hold.

x

Finally, the moment every mind slave on Earth had been waiting for happened. In fact, the whole situation (in their mentality of unreality) was rather entertaining to them. Komodo walked towards the front of the stage and announced, "You there… with the gun… put down the pistol and you may have a moment of my time."

Muhammad, seeming not to have been phased, still did as instructed.

"Do you expect some kind of uprising to occur after your alleged self-aggrandized act of martyrdom, or are you just plain senseless?" Asked Komodo, who was questioning just how long this could go on.

"The point is, Komodo, that I have got inside your mind. And if I can do it, so can someone else!"

Komodo wiped his mouth as if something funny had just been said.

"Although this is a good attempt at that- after hundreds of years of being alive, I must admit there have been much better attempts than this. Because if you haven't noticed, nobody has shown up and your life is still in my hands. If that is all, this was really a pathetic way of showing just how miniscule an uprising would be and exactly how easy it would be to extinguish it.

"The virus can't be stopped through a radio frequency... So, really?" Komodo readjusted his ankle-length dress. "If there is nothing more, I will kill you now. And I apologize, Venessa, but my time is short and you will have to be sacrificed."

Komodo motioned with his hands for the military to torch the bakery. Muhammad turned towards the camera and said, "The mind is a terrible thing to waste. If there is anyone out there listening, whether you are under the influence of Millennial 2084 or not, please form a resistance! Anyone who remains undiscovered who has not been exposed to the virus- continue to resist and be sustained by this act of courage! Know that we are not alone and that this WAR has only now officially begun."

As flames quickly rose around us, smoke filled my lungs. Venessa began screaming hysterically and Zeke opened the door to the attic, allowing us to clamber into the room. Yet, as useful an idea as that was, none of us had any means of seeking temporary relief on the roof because there was no opening to it. Either way, though, we were goners by fire or being shot; and so we slowly suffocated.

The fire below the attic became too intense to go back down to exit a window, where guns would be waiting. I wagered the pain from a gunshot would have been less excruciating than from the flames.

Before the carbon monoxide had us all gasping for our final breaths, Zeke had a panic attack. I lay down and said a prayer to Jesus before I died. The last thing I remember was a firefighter entering the attic through the flames below. He said he was going to help our team of insurgents to escape, and since we had absolutely no other option; we trusted him. I was the last to be discovered as I had rolled to the furthest wall to suck air out of a hole in the attic wall, which I had realized meant I would be more than likely to die because of the flames rather than the smoke.

The firefighter took me in his arms and covered me with a fire-resistant blanket. The figure wearing a fire suit quickly took off their helmet, and I saw it was Sid. He told me about the plan to crawl through the tunnel to safety and then, after placing his helmet back on, to my despair, he began pulling me downstairs into the flames where I became so overheated that I literally passed out. We continued retreating deeper into the house until he dragged my limp body into a hole that had been dug into the ground at the bottom of the house. Placing a harness around my waist and his, I finally awoke from my brief pass out.

Sid was the first to begin the journey through the tunnel. He fastened us all together with cable. Following Sid was Venessa, me, Zeke, Muhammad and finally Abdi. Even though our faces were covered by the portable oxygen apparatuses, breathing was considerably strenuous. The shaft, which had been dug via a tunnel boring machine that Sid would thereafter refer to as "the mole", was pitch black aside from the light we saw from Sid's flashlight.

We crawled arduously underneath the neighborhood Muhammad lived in for three miles until, after what felt like millennia, the six of us exited the tunnel. Once we had reached our destination, we were far enough away from the bakery to be undetected, yet close enough to see the building finished being consumed by flames. The fresh air stirred me and I worked to gather my senses.

CHAPTER 16

We found ourselves amid a lumber yard but had scant enough time to collect our surroundings. This was because Sid instructed each of us to run to the spaceship, which had been professionally camouflaged, one at a time to not draw awareness to ourselves.

Sid and I were the last to arrive in the spacecraft. Once I was inside, Orthopox and Jamie embraced us. Orthopox immediately received me with a warm bear hug.

"Pleased to see you all safe and in one piece! For heaven's sake, look at the state of your clothes... and your faces. They are covered with mud!" commented Jamie.

"I'd like to see you try to clamber through a three-mile-long tunnel under a rural region and not look like this!" replied Sid, amusedly.

"Well anyhow," declared Jamie without optimism ever leaving her face, "you all can wash up... oh, Arnold, this arm will require stitches! Sid, please attend to this. Everyone else, please freshen up in the locker room; sorry we only have one so please swallow your pride- not that you will need to honey," she added erotically while winking at Sid. Clearing her larynx with an "Ahem," Jamie went on, "Please familiarize yourself with the crew cabins and the lounge. We will be ready for takeoff within the hour!"

Everyone stood quietly for moments until Jamie added, "As captain of this ship and the person in charge of getting us to our next destination, it is pertinent for crew members to acknowledge with a 'YES SIR!'"

And so, the six of us returned with a "YES SIR" and even a salute to Jamie from Sid.

x

Sid and I, along with Zeke, Abdi, and Muhammad, undressed in the locker room. Upon seeing the dilemma Venessa faced, Jamie invited her to shower in the captain's quarters, which she accepted half-heartedly.

On the lower deck, Zeke and I took to showering next to each other. Though the other men suspected our attraction to each other, we did nothing more than glance at each other's exposed bodies. At first, the locker room was filled with laughter at the experiences that had just transgressed. Not long after we had all finished showering, besides Abdi who was last to finish showering because of having trouble removing the mask from his alien body, a serious conversation took place as we were getting dressed.

"Sid?" I inquired hesitantly, realizing that it had taken me up to this moment to ask the most obvious question.

He looked at me with an expression of pure joy, which was a recompense for being reunited. He was eager to boast, as was clear via his jubilant expressions during the shower, how he had finally found me and that the mission to save us had been a success.

"Yes?" replied Sid as he gestured for me to sit down on the bench so that he could finish stitching up my sliced arm.

I sat down next to him and watched as he numbed my arm with a gelatinous goo and used something like a fishhook to suture my flesh together. Afterward, Venessa brought down a sling from the med room and handed it to Sid while covering her eyes from seeing the naked men. Zeke was not bashful about how well-endowed he was in the reproductive arena.

Using one arm to buckle my pants as the other was in a sling, I continued with my query. Which was, "Where are we going?"

"To Svetlana, my lad! There is an underground resistance led by the eminent intellect of one ancient known as, 'The Rebel'. Your presence is requested by The Council as you are still, according to our books, a senator for Planet Earth- there has also been discussion of making you an ambassador, but as of right now that is not the key priority," explained Sid.

The talk of returning to Svetlana brought tears to my eyes. I recalled memories spent with Samuel. In fact, it was on Svetlana that we had lost our virginities together. At that moment, Zeke couldn't help but look curiously over at Sid and me as we embraced each other, being as happy to see each other as we were dismayed by the death of Sam. Of course, Zeke did not understand all this, but gave me a wink as he pulled on an undershirt and put on his button-down apparel.

With my arm now being medically attended to, at least with what could be made possible with Sid's competence, which was substantially more than one could ask for as a fugitive, I stood up and dried my tears with my sleeve. Turning towards Zeke in order to answer his questions that I interpreted by his facial expressions were inescapable, I instead abruptly and with a fearful urgency shouted at Sid.

"Wait! Hold everything! We cannot leave behind Queen Nubia and the other Norvegicans who are caught inside the work camp on Earth!"

Sid glanced at me with a nervous sensitivity that I translated as being owed to being lifted out of the trace our reunion had placed us back into the world of the intransigent opposition to Lord Komodo's tyranny.

"I am familiar with Queen Nubia. How else do you assume

I could pinpoint Orthopox? She had been very busy while on Earth. In fact, she is technically a renegade, as she escaped the work camp only four hours after arriving. Since then, she has been very busy communicating with the Council as they plot against the Space Rangers.

"Though, I must admit that before she reconnected with me, I was not conscious of the existence of the planet Zumumbufum. Of course, I knew of the System of Correction- but the name of Planet Zumumbufum was new to me," acknowledged Sid, as he quickly recovered his equanimity. I did not see some of the body expressions that Sid was expressing, which would have shown to me that though he was serene, much was troubling his mind.

During those moments, I later found out, what was bothering Sid most was the plan he had structured in his head with the help of other leaders in the resistance. The plan would complete what Jamie called "Phase One."

Sid knew the plan would either get everyone killed while giving Komodo more power to rule the galaxy (what was feared most was that it would soon because galaxies, plural). Either that or events would turn to the less likely alternative and the Milky Way would be freed of the Space Rangers.

What happened next was that I readjusted my body, which had become in a somewhat pleading position as my emotions had taken me into a bit of a frantic hysteria. My gut was telling me that leaving the planet Earth without the Norvegicans was the wrong thing to do. After all, they had been the ones who had negotiated with Malcolm to grant us free and safe passage back to Planet Earth while restoring my free will.

I recalled the night in the warehouse with perfect clarity. Queen Nubia had offered to tell Malcolm the exact nature of her shenanigans for releasing Gilgamesh from the chemical torture she subjected him to while attempting to find out what he knew.

Not only did she free Gilgamesh from the maniacal contraption, but the only workable way she could secure our passage back to Earth was by divulging the location of The Ancient Rebel, whose discovered location was the primary objective given to Malcolm by Komodo.

Of course, while I was still experiencing this event in my life, I considered how The Rebel was an outcast of her race simply because she wanted to create sentient life-forms and allow them to experience psychological freedom, as opposed to the other Ancients who were distrustful and had a dark desire to be worshiped.

Knowing the location of The Rebel Ancient was valuable enough information for Malcolm to agree to allow the Norvegicans safe passage to Earth. Komodo's goal in capturing the outlier of The Ancient's race would, as he expected, lead to the obtainment of technology that would place him on equal footings with the most intelligent beings in the galaxy.

Being that Samantha and I had followed all the rules, taken each dose of Millennial 2084 (to her knowledge), and graduated from the reeducation programming that instilled a belief in Lord Komodo as a divine being to offer absolute obedience to, it was convenient for both myself and Orthopox as well as the Norvegicans to take a ship to Earth together. It could even be said that in Malcolm's eyes, our party was so meager that any plan we could devise stood no chance of success.

As I explained this story to Sid, I mentioned how it was because of Queen Nubia and Gilgamesh that my wife Samantha and I had returned to my parents' house. I also mentioned how at the last minute Malcolm had informed the Norvegicans that although she would not break the agreement she'd made with Nubia, she and the other Norvegicans would be placed in a work camp upon landing on Earth and be forced to take the mind control serum. Her only compromise was that she would be released upon the capture of The Ancient Rebel, of whom was thought to be hiding with King Thaddeus in the secret underwater capital of Polunin, his home planet.

"Come on Arnold," said Sid as he gestured towards the staircase leading up into the navigation room. "I have something, or rather someone, to show you."

As we made steady strides up the stairs, Jamie and Venessa could be overheard talking in the captain's quarters as we entered the room with a multitude of computer panels and a large screen where the external views of reality taking place outside the ship could be seen.

Once upstairs, we were greeted by Queen Nubia.

"It is a delight to be healthy and in your presence once again, Arnold Fitzgerald," she elegantly announced while giving a nod to Sid, whom she had already been acquainted with.

"I imagine you have a lot of questions- questions you may know the answer to," she said while looking up to me. The cane she was holding made apparent her age, though her facial expressions, seen through gray fur, were jubilant and emanated the warm glow of youth.

"Yes ma'am, I mean… Your Highness," I stuttered as I felt I was near someone of a higher class and greater importance than myself.

"I appreciate the sentiment, but as someone who holds equal responsibility as part of this resistance, and as a senator and future ambassador of Earth, we must put aside ideas of status and our petty differences because of what is at hand. Understand, young man, that the well-being of my species is in as much jeopardy as yours," said the Queen of the Norvegicans.

At that moment, Zeke was heard taking a rough and uneven gait up the stairs. Seeming to have not seen the Queen because of her short stature, I walked to meet him just as his eyes were looking over the command room.

His eyes told me everything as I greeted him. I considered I saw his heart beating through his chest because of his excitement. Of course, the reason for this was that, apart from knowing Muhammad who had only just revealed his true physical identity for the first time while we were showering off the mud that our trudge through the underground tunnel had left on us, in fact, he had never in his life seen a spaceship before.

Zeke walked around asking questions in excited haste until his eyes met with Nubia, who had yet to finish her conversation with me.

"Mm... Arnold? Why is there a large mouse wearing a crown walking this way?" asked Zeke, unable to control his laughter as he questioned his sanity.

Zeke quickly realized that this was not a laughing matter as the Norvegican announced in the royal decree she was accustomed to, "My name is Queen Nubia."

The pronunciation of her introduction was said in a tone that made the room feel rich and her company something to be prized.

Zeke stood up straight and the grin on his face was replaced by an expression of humility and governed respect.

The Queen continued, "The Komodians have wrongly enslaved my species. I and the other members of this crew are all that is left of our culture. It is a pleasure to meet your acquaintance, Mr. Zeke."

Nubia looked at the three of us beseechingly, as if the very hope of her species and the future of the galaxy rested in our hands. During that same moment, Venessa and Jamie walked in with the gate and attire of astronauts preparing to leave for a lunar satellite; apparently, they had become good friends.

"Greetings crew!" said Jamie. "Please get prepared for the

takeoff. We will depart Earth shortly with the planet Svetlana as our destination!"

Suddenly, a Norvegican dressed in a woodland outfit and carrying a sword did a double flip over the security module, which stood waist-high.

"Eureka!" he shouted, and it soon became obvious to me, though no surprise to Jamie or Nubia, that the energetic ball of fury was Gilgamesh.

"Gilgamesh! You made it! When I saw how nervous Sid was when I mentioned you guys, I feared the worst!" I exclaimed joyfully.

"Yes, I made it! Silly! Who do you think could coax Orthopox out of your parents' house while he was still under the effects of Millennial 2084?" beamed Gilgamesh with great pride.

The smile widened on my face.

"But who... I mean... how did you ever find Jamie and Sid?" I wondered.

"Well, that's an easy one, Arnold. Queen Nubia has ties all around the galaxy. For the past several days, we have been communicating in secret. Things had to move with great speed and with precise agility in order to not be detected by the Space Rangers. The Rebel and King Thaddeus had to be moved to an underground bunker on Svetlana, where a few other council members have sought a place to devise a scheme that can stop this mental captivity.

"Queen Nubia and the rest of our crew who could make it out of the work camp have been meeting in confidence with what we are calling freedom fighters to get messages out that The Ancient Rebel is in danger- and what better place than right beneath the very eyes of the Space Rangers who have taken siege over Svetlana. In an underground bunker!" said Gilgamesh passionately.

"AND THAT'S WHY WE'RE GOING TO SVETLANA!!! WHOOO!" screeched Zeke, throwing his fists up in excitement.

As Jamie was motioning everyone to buckle in, I asked the one lingering question on my mind.

"How did King Thaddeus know where Sid was? In fact, where were you?" I asked.

"It is a long story Arnold..." said Sid thoughtfully.

"Yes, something to be discussed over dinner tonight as no information concerning the Council or The Rebel has been disclosed at this point; especially not over frequencies that can be tapped into. Although I've had many intuitions about what The Rebel might think and want, we will help her so I do not mind sharing," interrupted the benevolent queen.

CHAPTER 17

Venessa was the last to buckle. I later found out from Jamie that this was because she was still very uncertain about trusting us, as it would have been just as easy for her to request to be left on Earth. Yet, she was still heartbroken that the man she had worshiped since childhood had left her to burn alive in Muhammad's hiding place, which he had purposefully lit on fire knowing that she was trapped inside. All without even the slightest apology.

As if she were nothing, that a lifetime of service to this man amounted to her being nothing more than a nematode. In later years, Venessa would recall this time in her life as the exact moment she pondered these ideas and everything she had previously believed or been persuaded into thinking was true. Her entire mental frame of reference was questioned just as the ship was taking off, which was the story that made this mission famous.

In the dining hall, which was in the same cabin as the kitchen as Jamie's ship was of a customized one and stood like a miniature dwarf amongst larger vessels, we were all arriving at the dinner party. One by one we arrived at the scheduled time, as we had all been having leisure time since entering deep space navigation and turning the spaceship on autopilot.

Zeke and I had been hanging out together in our shared quarters. We took the time to talk and get to know each other better. We wanted to slow things down and get properly acquainted because of how fast things progressed sexually between us after we had met at Muhammad's upstairs apartment of the bakery.

Looking back on that evening, I remember listening to music from planets all over the galaxy and talking to Zeke about the adventures I had with Sam. I also told Zeke about how Sam died tragically, which was when he embraced me and returned the affectionate masculine warmth I longed for.

After my spiel on how I first became attracted to males and how my first love had been stolen from me, Zeke began telling me about his life as well. We had the room's machine bartender, named Beyoncé, make us fireballs as we discussed our histories and what this mission had at stake.

The story I found most interesting about Zeke's life is an integral part of this tale, so before going back to what took place at the dinner party on the way to Svetlana, I will first go into the night that changed my new friend's life forever.

x

The first confession from Zeke was that ever since the Space Rangers had invaded Earth, he had taken up the use of drugs, which turned into a toxic and expensive addiction. Of course, even people who had been poisoned with the Millennial 2084 virus could still experience physical addiction to a drug. Although any consumption of mind-altering substances did little to anyone infected with the virus, if the "Jellyfish Juice" which comprised members of King Thaddeus' species was consumed, it did in fact give a person an intense rush. Only, that type of drug was extremely expensive, and Zeke had wasted his entire inheritance from his grandfather on the drugs- including losing his house and all his friends.

Then one night, Muhammad had been out stealing automobile parts and taking money out of cars, which is when he discovered Zeke. Muhammad witnessed Zeke being kicked out of the back door of a nightclub because he had run out of money to pay for his Jellyfish Juice. Having borrowed drugs and promised to pay the dealer back, the dealer contacted the manager with whom he was good buddies and threw Zeke out the door. He was fortunate the virus prohibited a more violent result.

Alone and having no place to stay the night, his mind was feeling cold, which reminded him he needed a boost. Inside his leather jacket, he took out the Jellyfish Juice, which was contained in red capsules with big red XX's on them (symbolizing a reminder to the user of the highly illegal nature of the substance). He consumed the last of the uppers and sat down outside the door of the nightclub which stood next to the dumpster.

Now, you understand Muhammad did not simply steal car parts for the sake of saving money, though that was the main idea. Instead, he had been involved with a group of outlaws who united and met in secret, calling themselves intellectuals. This sporadically spread out and strategically chosen group of renegades was considered being reprobate by the Komodians. These people had either been given the antidote for the Millennial 2084 virus the Space Rangers were spreading in order to control humanity or they had simply avoided the virus altogether.

The Komodians knew there were many people out there who were not infected and those people were being hunted. Social media was being intensely monitored and people would be interrogated by police if they were detected behaving autonomously or if they looked contemplative, as anyone exposed to the virus would be inhibited from having independent volition of mind.

Escaping the detection of the Gestapo was not at all easy. In fact, now that the existence of the antibodies was known about by Lord Komodo, he began ordering blood screens that would detect whether the antibodies were present in someone's body, and if they were, the person would be forced to take stronger medication such as Soma for the rest of their lives.

So, one man whom Zeke told me went by the name of

Teko, who was at first a simple insurgent, tracked down the antidote and started an automotive operation- anything from large eighteen-wheelers to luxury sedans.

Teko would pay what he and Muhammad, who became friends in a roundabout fashion, called the "hoodwinked people", or people who were indoctrinated into the Komodian scheme of affairs, to deliver baked goods all over the United States. Tangentially, Queen Nubia had discovered someone who had taken the antidote, and through this person she tracked down Teko. It was through him and the involvement with other individuals who were freed from the shackles of conformity under Lord Komodo that she was able to contact Sid. Yet, that part of the story we will come back to later.

Within the lining of the packaging of the food made in the bakery was the vaccination for the Millennial 2084 virus. Zeke worked part time at the bakery, but mostly, he stayed in an apartment by himself where he got high on Jellyfish Juice or had sex with hoodwinked guys he met through the internet; somewhat of a letdown, according to Muhammad, although he was honestly not very surprised.

Zeke portrayed the story of how the Gestapo had started blood screening people for the antibodies of the virus and what happened to the ones who got caught and refused to take medication This was how he heard of the planet Zumumbufum, though he didn't know the planets name until I told him. His words painted pictures that played out clearly in my imagination.

So as Zeke, to get back on track, was taking his drugs that night outside the nightclub, he spent the night in the alley. In his high and euphoric state brought on by the drugs he had taken, he told me how he knew the drugs came from the planet Polunin of a jellyfish species. The drugs were, in fact, the refined chemical substances derived from the jellyfish-like sentient species of Polunin. He was not aware that the species was sentient until he and I had this discussion. He shed a few tears as I informed him how the Space Rangers had King Thaddeus' species on the extreme verge of extinction.

Of course, I was very interested in this story and I enjoyed spending time with my new friend. As we sat comfortably next to each other on Jamie's ship, I relished the fact that Zeke was a rare breed of man who both felt comfortable not wearing a shirt and also looked physically attractive. Anytime he stood up to do things like getting another drink from Beyoncé, admire the artwork on the walls, or when he tired of sitting and moved over to the bed, the bulge in his sweatpants got my attention. My mind wandered off toward what we might do later this evening or after the dinner party.

Zeke's young adult voice was music to my ears. As I continued to hear about how he spent his time after he was released from psychological slavery, his passion for the mission we were embarking on this story was beyond apparent.

So anyway, the story goes Muhammad had been watching him as he was stealing money, jewelry, and parts out of cars. He saw the police pull up to the alley with their flashing blue lights and began arresting him for not paying his tab at the bar. Only then, to what can only be described in my eyes as luck that comes only once in a thousand generations, Zeke did not have any of the illegal drugs on him, as only elite Komodians had permits for the Jellyfish Juice in his possession. He also did not have the antibodies in his bodily system.

Muhammad intervened just as the manager of the nightclub and the police, who were also hoodwinked humans, were placing him under arrest. Zeke imitated Muhammad's Arabic accent with precision, as it was a night that changed his life forever.

"Excuse me, please, but may I inquire why my friend here is under arrest?" asked Muhammad.

Zeke said that his eyes must have been so dilated that the light from the police blinded him. Simultaneously, the drugs made his mind feel as if it were clinging to reality by a thin string and kept it moving in several directions.

"For not paying his bill sir," replied the officer, who had been educated to believe that having any sort of personality that was not part of the standardized protocol that was the state of affairs during the reign of Komodo, indicated criminal behavior.

The officer placed handcuffs on Zeke, which was when Muhammad again intervened.

"Excuse me officers, but my friend had money to pay- he simply left his money in the car, and I was on the way back in to bring it to him," said Muhammad deceitfully.

Zeke described that although the Millennial 2084 virus would have usually made him unable to not comply with an officer, which included not telling the truth, he thought that the psychotropic drugs he was taking were so good that he agreed to take the money and handed it over to the manager- $350 to be exact. The bill for the drugs was actually much more than that, but the manager had lied to the officers to begin with because he wanted the money so that he and the dealer could buy more of the Jellyfish Juice to get high with. It explains why the manager could also lie to the hoodwinked officers without having been given the antidote.

The manager left with a berated attitude, and the officers quickly went along with him. To our great relief, Muhammad was not tested for the antibodies- which was a courageous act on his behalf that could have otherwise ended very badly.

"Well, boy, my name is Muhammad. I run a bakery business." He said, only being half honestly. "If you'd like, we could use your help to manage it," inquired Muhammad nonchalantly.

Zeke described how his cognitive experience made the

world appear in a prism-like array of colors. Since he had no other alternative solution, Zeke agreed. The next several days comprised intense detoxing from the drugs as well as an injection of the antibodies, which kept him in a nervous haste and completely soaked with sweat.

"And the rest is history," finished Zeke.

I crawled over to Zeke's bed, which was next to mine, and gave him a big kiss. He returned it in a way that I knew was not only about our sexual attraction, of which there was plenty, but because of his genuine interest in me; it was the beginning of a beautiful relationship.

CHAPTER 18

Zeke and I dressed in some formal attire that the spaceship's computer designed for us. After that, we made our way to the kitchen/dining area, which was close to our suite. Then, upon entering the mess hall, our newly formed crew greeted us, including Orthopox who had been assisting Sid with preparing the meal.

"How do you like your noodles, boys? You have the choice between spicy and extra spicy! Both, I might add, are especially tasty," said Sid with a bourgeoisie enunciation.

Having tasted Sid's cooking in the past, I knew it would be delicious, but I was certain I did not want the "extra" spicy. Zeke and I both decided on the safer dish that was less spicy. Queen Nubia accepted her position at the head of the dinner table, albeit not an enormous table. The noodles and homemade bread were bountiful. Orthopox, who wore a hairnet, keeping in the pink hair which had grown back to cover his entire body, served the meal before receiving his own chair between Sid and myself.

Before we began eating, Captain Jamie delivered the customary gratuities to the chefs and to everyone's respectful spiritual affiliations. Apart from the sumptuous spice noodles and homemade bread, we also had a few bottles of authentic Svetlananian plum wine, and not the kind that was synthesized by the computer. At the end of the dinner party, there were still several unopened bottles left in the cabinets. Though simple and conveniently prepared- apart from the sauce for the noodles that Sid expertly whipped up- the supper was far from modest.

Our company made the meal appear as if it were from a lavish and swank restaurant; our table manners reflected that attitude. We each ate more than our fill, which was topped off by some homemade peach cobbler for dessert, prepared with real peaches from Earth, I might add. Zeke and I gave most of our attention to each other until the meal was over when we spoke about serious business.

"Captain Jamie, when is this vessel scheduled to land?" inquired Queen Nubia.

"We have thirty-six hours and nine minutes at warp nine," answered the ship's computer without being asked.

"Thank you, Peter Pan," said Jamie pretentiously.

"You named your ship Peter Pan?" asked Zeke.

"Actually, the ship chose the name for himself and also identified as the male gender. Yes, in fact, as a fully conscious being, the Council of Planets of the Milky Way Galaxy considers certain programs, such as Peter, as fully sentient life-forms. Peter certainly has his own personality, such as when he speaks out of turn!" replied the captain teasingly.

"Eh-hem?" uttered Queen Nubia to redirect our attention. "What requires to be reviewed is what will take place once we arrive at Planet Svetlana," she said with a coherent mind and a determined approach for us to work together. A desire which drew on her energy that was dedicated to resolving the dilemma the Space Rangers had put on her planet and dozens of others in this quadrant alone.

The Queen demanded her planet be liberated from the Komodian autocracy. These Space Rangers had pillaged their livelihoods and enslaved the minds of her people and my own. I understood her desire to find a solution.

"Why don't we come back to the business at hand," declared Queen Nubia with a display of authority. "I would like to update you all about some details of what has taken place before discussing the mission at hand."

The supper was officially over as what she said penetrated our ears, and we concentrated on what the monarch was revealing.

"As you all may have gathered, after my people and I were placed in a work camp on Earth, I single-handedly escaped by waking up during the late hours of the night and discreetly burrowing under a wall. Guards quickly caught sight of me, and I was shot at with machine guns..." added Queen Nubia.

"Did you sustain an injury?" asked Captain Jamie during the pause.

"No ma'am, I did not, but thank you for the concern," replied Nubia. "As I was saying, what happened then was that I tracked down a tail of people who had been vaccinated against the virus- by using my acute observation. To make a long story short, I used a satellite owned by a young scientist who went by the name of Stephen to contact Sid who owed me a favor," the Queen paused again.

"How did you know how to contact him?" asked Muhammad.

"I did what any rational being would do who owned an interplanetary communications device. I dialed his private telephone number and left a message telling him about the situation with me and my crew."

"Okay, okay, that makes sense, but what was Sid doing while you were contacting him?" questioned Muhammad.

"And how did you and Sid know each other to begin with?" I inquired.

There was a great interest in this question amongst us,

excluding Sid and Nubia. We were all very intrigued by how this plan had come together so perfectly. Though, the exact nature of the social protocol we were going to follow once we were near The Ancient Rebel was still unknown.

Zeke and I whispered together with Muhammad and Abdi about why The Rebel Ancient had stayed on Svetlana. What was really going on in the outer reaches of the galaxy, and... what was going on in galaxies where The Ancient alien species had navigated using their supposed advanced technology?

Suddenly Peter Pan, the ship's computer, interrupted the chatter going on at the table. "ATTENTION PASSENGERS," said the boisterous sound emanating from the ship's sound system. "If you would like me to design a program that will allot each of you the opportunity to ask your questions one at a time or alert you to when it is your turn to speak, I can easily make those arrangements."

"Thank you, Peter, but that will not be necessary, as we have everything under control," rejected Captain Jamie.

"Very well. Awaiting next orders," replied the ship's computer.

Venessa stood up and took an authoritative stance. "I, for one, am conscious of the limited time and psychological resources that we have and plan to dedicate every ounce of energy to defeating Lord Komodo. We must put a stop to the spread of this virus and to putting a direct halt to all re-education that is taking place on Zumumbufum and other planets, such as those you all might have not heard of including Planet DiNapoli's, Planet Iridate, and the species who inhabit the gas giant planet orbiting the star Sirius A called Milionis."

Venessa's assertiveness gained her the attention and respect of her crewmates, with her scaly hands on the table and shoulders hunched; more had been going on in her mind than anyone noticed. Once it became conspicuous how dramatically her allegiance had changed, the entire crew of Jamie's ship realized they had neglected to even ask her how she was feeling since the ship departed.

Queen Nubia took advantage of the moment's hesitation and asked Sid to fill everyone in on how he and she had met each other's acquaintance, as well as about what he knew concerning the mission at hand.

Venessa, sweat dripping down her face in a psychological experience of existential excitement, slowly sat down to collect her consciousness, but with a fierce passion remaining in her eyes.

Sid stood up in his diplomatically expressed haughtiness and informed the crew about what they needed to know. His eagerness to express every detail with scientific precision had him practically standing on the tip of his toes.

With the expressions concerning the exact details, Sid apprised the crew of how the Space Rangers, now known as the Komodians since the official arrival of Lord Komodo on Earth, originally came to Planet Earth as a part of the Milky Way Galaxy Council of Planets. The council has since become split in the matter of whether to support the Space Rangers. Of course, if it is not crystal clear by this point, Lord Komodo's regime is far from anything a rational political organization would condone.

"However, the matter comes strictly down to a vote..." He sighed and cursed the flawed nature of the council, which was a representative democracy. "... many of the council members have fueled their planets' infrastructure with Xubuntos, which is mined on Zumumbufum. Or else they have been driven into political terror and are too afraid to lose their own psychological freedom because of the possibility of their own planet being included in the list of approved planets to infect with the virus. I, for one, am against such a list; however, denying that the council has not put in the final vote would be foolish.

"Which was why, post my escape after I was captured by Malcolm and left to die on an uninhabitable desert planet within her own solar system, The System of Correction, we- knowing the council was assembling in secret on Svetlana- set out to find Arnold. This was because Arnold continues to have the reputation, autonomy, and authority to cast a vote within the council chamber. It continues to press me that the way the Space Rangers are going to win this war is because the council will never have the opportunity for all 152 of the council members to cast a vote on this issue. This means our political unions will disintegrate and the war will blunder off into chaos.

"Of course..." continued Sid. "... things changed after the information The Ancients shared with us during the first contact on September 24, 2090, along with dozens of council member life-forms from all across the Orion Arm of the Milky Way- that The Rebel Ancient had planted seeds of life on these planets and let them evolve without the use of the mechanized virus which she had helped to develop. Having expected none of the planets within the Orion Arm to achieve space travel, The Ancients had allowed The Rebel to conduct these experiments.

"Jamie and I, who had been the one to rescue me from the desert with the help of The Rebel, embarked on the journey back to Planet Earth in response to Queen Nubia's distressed telephone call. Yes, I was at home when Nubia called, but I did not answer because I at first did not know who it was, and further did not pick up once I recognized who it was because I did not want the enemy to get any additional information about my liberation. At the moment the Queen of the Norvegicans called, I was putting together a plan to rescue Arnold and Orthopox from the System of Correction, which was the last place I had known to be their whereabouts.

"It was largely a matter of coincidence that Arnold and his new friends, who are now part of our crew, were discovered on television in an effort to sway the public's opinion and thwart

Lord Komodo's sinister scheme."

Sid was providing the team who were sitting around the dining table with details that painted a picture within each of their mental visions. When he paused, I asked a question that had been plagued me since Sid was separated from Orthopox and me.

"What did Malcolm want from you and what means did she use to get it?" I asked.

Sid explained how Malcolm wanted to know how Jamie and Thaddeus used the depiction of the alien constellations to find the planet The Ancients inhabited. "She diabolically shredded me of everything I once felt proud of and used re-education techniques, drugs, and violence to get every shred of information she could."

"Why didn't they just warp to the planet?" Sid said, mimicking Malcolm's stern and authoritarian voice.

"King Thaddeus said it would not be wise," Sid responded, portraying how he spoke of Malcolm's desperation. "His species designed communication and navigational technology far exceeding any of the known species to have achieved," explained Sid. "Truth be told, Thaddeus' ability to detect which planet had the constellations that matched the ones on the map is unsurpassed even by The Ancients. In fact, one reason they helped us was because of how impressed they were in King Thaddeus being able to send a signal in a timely manner, somehow exceeding the speed of light," said Sid, proud of his colleague.

"Then," continued Sid, "in a tone so sinister, maniacal, and diabolical... She demanded I tell her where King of the Pelage, the oceanic organism with long tentacles could be found, as they had searched the planet repeatedly and found no trace of the king nor any kind of scientific laboratories. Her tone was so foreboding that I had no choice but to tell her because I feared she was unmatched in her ability to think of new ways to torture me."

X

Jamie interjected, "Sid calculated our inevitable retreat because he knew we were aware he had been captured. By the time Malcolm's fleet arrived at the hidden underwater city known as Prism City, King Thaddeus and myself, as well as the remaining Pelages people, had already been in contact with The Ancients.

"If it had not been for the expertise of the Pelages scientist Ramos Destin Uphanivan, constructing a map of every star in the galaxy as well as their orbiting planets would never have been possible. This scientific genius could not only make the star map of every star in the Milky Way Galaxy but also invented new technology. Technology that could send an electronic signal from the Orion Arm we all live to any other of the four arms of the Milky Way."

Jamie continued talking to the group who, now having finished dessert, continued to be present in each other's company around the dinner table. "When Thaddeus, Ramos, and I signaled the same location, The Ancients responded from the first time, this time we got a timely response, only taking a matter of a few days. It was that we convened with The Ancient who went by the appellative of The Rebel.

"After receiving our distress signal, she returned communications describing how she would arrive in Prism City within a matter of hours. She was a tall, gray alien with enormous black eyes who wore a simple sash around her waist and breasts. She appeared out of a portal that she opened with an artificial star mechanism that fit around her wrist and fingers.

"Being as old as modern human sapiens, as her species does not die except by a physical injury, she told us how she was a scientist who experimented with the development of the Millennial 2084 virus, and so she felt like it was her responsibility to resolve this issue," Jamied reminisced as she continued.

"She made plans with us to use the safe house on Svetlana. The Rebel Ancient quickly began making plans of how to go about inviting council members to the safe house, starting with those whose allegiance was going to be with her cause. This was advertised as her side being the coalition against the egomaniac Lord Komodo.

"When apprised of the situation about Sid's whereabouts were unknown, The Rebel used her teleportation device that existed around her wrist to travel to the Komodian Correctional planets to find him. Being that she is a tenderhearted telepath, The Rebel searched for Sid's soul, or the essence of his presence, as she began visiting the most logical places that he could be in.

"Before embarking on the journey to locate Sid, the amicable Rebel said she would let us know when he was found but that her teleportation mechanism would not have enough energy to carry them both back to the safe house in Svetlana. In the meantime, prior to retreating to the underground bunker at Svetlana, we destroyed the scientific equipment before we left. All of Ramos Destin Uphanivan's work was lost in all its entirety.

"As the inventor and scientific genius had already been taken... and I should say the way it happened was that he was leaving his laboratory along with a group of scientists that were his team when, as usual, he avoided all the predictable traps that commonly occurred and got his fellows captured and turned into pharmaceuticals. Except this time, one specific Venetian bounty hunter known by the alias of "Wombat" (who was a species from the planet Venetia, which is a planet completely covered in rain forest) who was aware of Ramos' genius and was jealous and wanted to take him and exchange him for what he thought of as promised treasure."

Jamie continued the dinner party conversation, "Ramos knew keenly that someone had been watching him come and go from work, during which time the poaching of his species became something like deer experience during hunting season. Except the Pelages were more organized about it, and to keep the people of their world calm, their navigational systems were used to ensure they made it to work on time. Ramos' work was in Prism City, but he lived outside the city limits.

"Getting into work required swimming through hidden passages constructed to avoid being captured and killed. They believed that someone would help them, as no weapons existed on their planet for them to defend themselves with and that one day the poaching would be over.

"Yet Ramos left his guard down as he felt safe with his posse of scientists as they made their way to the university, they were employed to use their library, which was when the hunter swam out from above the entrance of the secret passage and murdered him with a simple fishing spear, which was uncommon as most Pelages were caught in large numbers using nets and electrical charges.

"Technology was lost that we may never have again and which could have been used to defeat those in favor of establishing Komodo as a galactic dictator if the odds would not have been stacked against us. His death occurred after destroying all the equipment and evidence pertaining to star maps and far-distance space travel, which was not far away from being able to jump from the Orion arm to the Perseus arm of the Milky Way, which is where The Ancients' planet exists."

Jamie digressed, and so I raised my hand to ask how Sid had been found.

Sid's answer was long-winded and went something like this, "When the Komodians discovered I had been honest and basically had almost no chance of surviving the injuries I sustained, they did me a courtesy and dropped me off on an uninhabitable desert planet. They left me with a gallon of milk, which I had to drink fast because it would have soured, and for days after that, I recycled my urine. After wading through the sand without sleep for four days, I found shade on the side of an enormous cliff. It was there I knew I was going to die. I admitted I was defeated and accepted my fate.

"When I heard the familiar voice of an Ancient, whose sound I could identify from the first encounter we had with them, I thought it was the effect of being scorched by the sun for those four days or because I had been drinking my urine.

"Once I realized one of them was actually looking for me, I shouted, 'Yes! Here I am! My luck has changed! The tables have turned! I have the chance to live once again, and oh how I will cherish every moment!'" shouted Sid, whose face was as red as a ripe tomato and with parched lips.

"It was The Rebel who appeared through a portal in front of me in that desert land where I had found shade. Wearing her sash, she looked carefree and greeted me like I was an old friend.

"'I am here to rescue you from certain death and take you back to your home world where your strategic intelligence is much needed,' said The Rebel Ancient. Then she held out her hand to me and I felt my mind move.

"When I opened my eyes, I was fully dressed, and the injuries I sustained from being in a toxic relationship with Malcolm were healed. In front of me, I was welcomed by many of my old acquaintances I had met as a diplomat. Also amongst the bunch were Thaddeus and Jamie. It was that night though that I snuck out of the safe house to visit the apartment I had on Svetlana, and it was then, as a matter of coincidence- just like meeting each of you for the first time was- I heard the phone ring and listened to Queen Nubia's voicemail.

"We were already preparing before Queen Nubia's distress call, which I wasn't expecting to come from Earth of all places and did not answer because I did not want her to notice the details of the rescue mission in case doing so would pose a threat to the success of the mission. At the moment the Queen of the Norvegicans called, I was putting together a plan to rescue Arnold and Orthopox from somewhere in The System of Correction, more specifically Zumumbufum. After the call, I knew to return to Earth," explained co-captain Sid.

"With the new destination, we put together a two-man crew comprising Captain Jamie and myself. We went to Arnold's home after rescuing Queen Nubia and her people, remembering where it was from our previous visit, hoping he and Orthopox would be there. When Arnold was revealed to be missing, we found ourselves at another dead end. The only reason we discovered the exact whereabouts of Arnold was another matter of chance. We witnessed Venessa on the television, and at the last minute when the house was being lit on fire, the camera spun around and we briefly glimpsed Arnold and knew we could track his location. We had to work quickly to save everyone from the fire."

"How did you ever escape the wrath of a creature with no sense of remorse?" wondered Abdi as he sipped Svetlanian wine through his insectoid mouth.

I was keenly aware of the most probable solution before it was announced, but decided not to voice my opinion, since Jamie was prepared to explain anyway.

Jamie responded to Abdi for a few minutes, "Many of the Milky Way Council members had already gathered in the renovated underground safe-house on Svetlana, disguised as an old closed down coal mine, something that hadn't been used for probably four hundred years. Once the council members who were using the facility as a refuge from tyranny found out Sid, one of the most famous diplomats, had been placed in police custody, their minds began concocting a plan to exonerate him of his charges. Since the Space Rangers did not go through the proper bureaucratic process for arresting a member of the Council of Galactic Peace, it became apparent that the Space Rangers now needed to be convicted of breaking the peace. Yet, as this process began, the council members knew that taking this route would not only mean the Komodians were criminals, but that they had declared war."

During the pause, Sid cleared his throat and entered back into the conversation. "After Malcolm got all the information, she wanted out of me and more, they left me in the desert on one of the uninhabitable Komodian planets which orbit Alpha Centauri. The Space Ranger's solar system is called 'The System of Correction' because, as one of the species who joined the council it it's youth, they had agreed to reform criminals throughout the Orion Arm. Hoping that through education and behavioral modification programming the criminals could return to their planet with no type of additional action necessary. The council of planets had agreed to use that solar system to help criminals reintegrate back into society; yet, often experimental procedures were performed by the Komodians because they wanted to appear like they were successful at their work.

"Many investigations took place until the Millennial 2084 virus was discovered on a planet in the outer reaches of the Orion Arm. All investigations towards the Space Rangers were dropped when the 2084 virus was approved by the Milky Way Council of Planets to be used to cure violent criminals. Not long after that, to end a war, the council approved the use of it on an entire planet who were said to be the aggressors, but the vote only met the quota by one senator. This task was performed by the Komodians, as they were already familiar with how to best use the virus."

Queen Nubia answered our quizzical expressions with, "The virus was discovered by the Armodafians during an approved mission of scientific inquiry. It was discovered on a planet that took three generations to find and retrieve data from. It is the furthest point of the Orion Arm of our galaxy that has been reached. The planet was named Plecostomus, or 'Pleco' for short, because the creatures inhabiting that planet resembled a fish that goes by that name on Earth.

"All the life-forms on Plecostomus were discovered to be infected with the virus, now known as Millennial 2084. This virus was not native to the planet because of the presence of nanotechnology, and whatever advancements they made were primitive at best. Whoever had brought the virus had abandoned them. We now know that The Ancients wanted to see how a species infected with the virus would develop- the result was the occurrence of de-evolution. More so, there were hardly any cognitive abilities to speak of as the organisms actually became deformed and lost their cognitive abilities, appearing slug-like and feeding off deposits of fossil fuels, which at this point can only sustain them for decades."

Queen Nubia continued, "This arm of the Milky Way had become decimated by endless competition over resources that could have easily been shared evenly, and so the Council of Planets for Galactic Peace, which most of us in this room sit on, authorized the relentless Komodian Space Rangers to use the virus which was found to oppress free will and therefore make managing people easier.

"Yet, what was first only supposed to be a harmless intervention, after Lord Komodo rose to greater power, and afterwards when his first followers and later his entire species called themselves Komodians, they used the virus to subjugate worlds to the autocratic rule of their divine leader. The council hoped that only species who chose war and destruction over the ability to show love and compassion would have this problem dealt with, but it soon got out of hand and now dozens of planets have lost their cognitive agility to express free will," expounded Queen Nubia of the Norvegicans.

Jamie took up where the Queen left off to finish telling everyone at the dinner party what was necessary to know. We were all ready to leave and go back to our rooms for the night, but we stayed and listened due to the importance of topic. "The handful of council members who have formed a coalition in the underground bunker disguised as an old coal mine on Svetlana, where we will be in a matter of hours, are but a fraction of the council who still live in denial that the Space Rangers will not use the viral weapon against them. These are frightful times for everyone, and the Komodians have the upper hand."

Sid seemed satisfied with the explanation that was given, though I still found it puzzling why having Samuel Yellowstone and myself appear to the council would have helped at all. Yet, I figured it was simply improvised behavior on Sid's behalf. Samuel and I were appointed as council members, or senators as some called us, as we were a couple of the few remaining cognizant human beings able to use free will to exist. After all, the fate of humanity and life on dozens of other planets all rested on the matter of a vote- I think Sid knew this all along, and judging from our character, he knew we had pure spirits filled with love for each other.

I think Sid knew this all along and that it never had even the slightest notion to do with Samuel and I being in love with each other, apart from knowing that deep down inside, our souls were as altruistic as Nelson Mandela. It was simply a numbers game, and Sid needed more.

"Remember that originally Jamie and Thaddeus signaled The Ancients' planet and, although the signal was received within a matter of hours, a reply was not given for twelve months. It wasn't until mid-year of 2089AD that the response was detected by King Thaddeus' team, which was all but what was left of his species. The Space Rangers collected the Pelages' tentacles and converted the proteins within into a drug called Jellyfish Juice which was consumed widely in the Komodian solar system but also, although not legal on Earth, by people willing to pay a steep price. This caused King Thaddeus to watch as his entire race was eaten, often alive, and now only a handful of Pelages are left," Sid stated somberly.

Zeke could visibly be seen becoming sick to his stomach. It made sense as he was a prior addict of the Jellyfish Juice made of the people of Polunin who King Thaddeus had benevolently led and taken care of. The same species had developed advanced communication systems and erected enormous and beautiful architectural structures made of their own saliva, a few dozen of whom were en route to other planets and of whom were too scared to return to their peaceful ocean world. Their race had never developed a weapon besides those that were used during civil wars in the old days. Therefore, they were helplessly brought to the brink of extinction.

CHAPTER 19

Later that night, I consoled Zeke, who I noticed became depressed when that subject came up. He felt great remorse over his addiction to consuming a sentient life-form, as I would later find out through his description of the night terrors he often had in our early years. I spent many a night listening to his passionate declarations that "somehow and one day" he would help King Thaddeus and contribute to establishing strong and mutually beneficial relationships between planets in the Orion Arm of the Milky Way. Thoughts which I helped to encourage with my enthusiasm for the positive nature that could take place in politics. My optimism for having hope in politics inspired Zeke, who wanted us to continue living the type of life we had experienced with the help of our new alien friends.

"And who knows, perhaps humanity or another species in the Orion Arm will one day soon reach a level of cognitive maturity that would be respected by The Ancients. If we can establish that we are worthy as a species and prove to The Ancients that we can use space travel technology that will take us past the furthest we've traveled, then at each planet we arrive at I could even help the galactic community in establishing political teamwork... isn't that something like a diplomat or federal agent?" thought Zeke.

"It would be nice. I'm not sure what you could call that line of work, but Sid could probably help us. Together, we could see other worlds, and with your new respect for sentient life, our ability to use our minds for good is practically unstoppable," I mentioned, becoming excited by his enthusiasm to be a reformed, good Samaritan.

"And when we either discover or are given the opportunity to travel to other galaxies by The Ancients', we can further our collective efforts to bring the creatures of the universe into an era where we work together to increase the quality of our lives for ourselves and other people!" beamed Zeke later that night as he pranced around gaily in his USA boxer briefs.

I would gush at how Zeke would so adamantly feel the desire to make up for his crime of consuming sentient life to get high. Then, with an expression that was the epitome of guilt, he confessed he had known before the first time he tried the Jellyfish Juice to get high that he was consuming the by-product of an intelligent life-form who had been murdered. He had made the same mistake time and time again and felt shamed, as well as a great sense of remorse.

At dinner though, picking up on the vibe that Zeke was putting out, Sid placed his hand on Zeke's shoulder and gave it a good squeeze. Both of the men know Zeke felt remorse and that he probably could never live with himself were Malcolm to have killed King Thaddeus and his remaining and faithful people. All that could be hoped for now was for Thaddeus to reclaim his planet and bring his citizens back to Prism City to begin the repopulation process in a new era of peace and prosperity.

x

Sid would later tell Zeke during an encounter on Svetlana something that would stick with him. "Heroes are not all perfect, not like you see in the comics. Sometimes a hero is simply someone who has stopped hurting other people or the environment and takes a step in the better direction, one of good nature and a healthy mind as opposed to the one he had while living in sin. A hero is a person who not only has changed his nature or habits but also who has learned their lesson," Sid would say.

"Seeing pain or devastation would never settle well with

a good man. His greed, pride, or self-involvement may sway a good man off the path of righteousness, but he can't go on living in sin forever and for a good reason. A good man may find temporary value in doing evil. The most popular philosophy of my planet, which differs from the path I am going to show you, states that those living in sin will be given great fortunes and people will be forced to say aloud that he is a good man and deserves his political power. Undoubtedly though, soon the criminal whose life has become built on lies, deceit, and self-righteousness will find his world falling to pieces.

"I've seen it a half-dozen times. Men who become very popular, like Lord Komodo, who have gained a lot of power but either inwardly or socially, that person's life will crumble because, contrary to what may be popular to believe, evil does not prosper for long," said Sid who was leading up to his main message.

"So, you're talking about karma... right?" asked Zeke.

"Well, a person who has everything will not easily turn from his evil ways. He will convince people he is a good man so that he can continue to live like a wretched crook. Muhammad told me the story of how, in your case, you hit rock bottom when you ran out of money to afford to get high. Hitting rock bottom always happens when you are not living altruistically and being aware of how your actions affect the well-being of people and the environment.

"However, you did not hit rock bottom because you withdrew from drugs; you are hitting rock bottom now because instead of contributing to the extinction of an entire race of people, you should have done the right thing and helped these people in need. It is from rock bottom that our eyes see through visions of guilt and shame how our ways have corrupted our sight and torn our humanity away from our very souls.

"Yes, I contend that the genuine heroes are those who have

made mistakes but have learned from them and made the choice to be a better person than they were the day before. An authentic hero has experienced mental anguish because his conscience is telling him or her they are not the person who should have made the mistake that they did; lost their way; got off the tracks; took a wrong turn; left the path indicative of a mentality that can be legitimately called the way a good man thinks... and so on and so forth. You get it.

"A true hero is like someone you will one day be able to call yourself Zeke- someone who has experienced the turmoil that takes place in the mind after one comes to terms that there is a righteous way to live and that they have not been living that way. Many people have good spirits, but those who can help share the forgiveness of Christ no longer have to live with the guilt of who they were before accepting their salvation and deciding to live in the righteous way that makes God happy to call us His children," said Sid who thereafter asked Zeke if he wanted to accept Jesus Christ as his savior. Although Sid was not a priest, he took a handful of water and baptized Zeke in the name of Jesus after he accepted the invitation.

That was a conversation Zeke would never forget. Because, through reading scripture and being Christ-like, Zeke bounced back from his life of crime. Zeke suffered from a crime of conscience until Sid shared his personal testimony with him- and this did not occur until years after the contents of this book had long passed and become history.

x

Muhammad, who had finished eating his noodles, was prompted to ask a question. "Why did it take an entire year for The Ancients to respond?" He still looked odd and unfamiliar because he was not wearing his Arab disguise, and so his face appeared like a grasshopper, although still humanoid. Also, when he dropped the inauthentic accent, he sounded somewhat musical, like an individual from a place I had never seen or heard of, almost like he was out of a fairytale. I figured it belonged well to whichever planet he was from.

"From what we gathered from meeting with The Ancients on the first occasion, it took them time to decide if they wanted to get involved. The Rebel has been waiting to fill us in on the rest of the details until we arrive at the safe-house on Svetlana. Basically, they weren't sure if they wanted to get involved with galactic politics. If it hadn't been for the advanced communication ability of the Pelages, the political debates on Atlantis would have never taken place. The Rebel informed me and the other council members within the underground bunker on Svetlana of the name of her planet during the conversation that took place when we first met officially," said Captain Jamie.

"This all sounds like bullshit to me," declared Abdi. "Why the hell would someone from this Atlantis planet be hiding in a bunker?"

"Because she wants to save the intellectual creatures that she created!" Jamie returned defensively.

"How the fuck did she create us? Who the fuck created her!" shouted Abdi who had drunk too much wine, unable to maintain a filter between his thoughts and lips.

Pretty soon the entire crew began arguing, including Orthopox, whose squeals I could hear above all the rest.

Captain Jamie pressed a button on her electronic watch which ordered Peter Pan, the ship's computer, to gas the room. Of course, she placed a small device between her nostrils so that the gas would not affect her.

A fine pink mist filled the room, and suddenly the crew began laughing. Yes indeed, Jamie had filled the room with laughing gas. I don't know what planet that strand of laughing gas derived from, but never in my entire life- and I am eighty-seven years old as I write this- had I laughed so hard my body ached that bad. The hilarious nature that must only be apparent to comic geniuses became apparent to me in those moments. As I looked at whom I was finishing sharing a meal with, their facial expressions reflected my own, and suddenly the simple fact that we were laughing became funny for the sake of being funny; then we each laughed for different reasons.

Queen Nubia was humorously reminiscing over the ironic nature of the relationship that already existed between The Rebel Atlantean and herself. Even though they had not even met in person yet, the vision of introducing herself as a queen to someone who had lived as long as she was hysterical. Though the effects of the gas were only temporary and she would later compose herself, the experience left a lasting impression.

After an hour of laughing, Venessa had experienced more than she could stand. It was a good thing the effects of the gas lasted only an hour because she became exhausted from finding humor in her own stupidity. What was most comical of all, while under the influence of laughing gas, was the fact that she had believed Lord Komodo cared about her.

Near the end of the hour, Captain Jamie came back into the room. Zeke and I were still chuckling over how it could really be possible that we were falling in love. In fact, our unending laughter was of a joyous type that resulted in us unabashedly kissing in front of everyone else.

Muhammad's laughter was more of a sarcastic type and was focused on how unrealistic the ideologies of the political leaders in this war seemed. He strolled the halls reminiscing on how absurd it was for a situation like this to be happening on this large of a scale.

Sid was busily engaged with his own reflections and he would later report, after the laughing gas wore off, about how serious his role in this war was. He laughed until the blood vessels in his face bulged outward. What he thought was funny was how completely crucial what we were doing to impact the outcome of this war truly was. That the people in this war took their roles so seriously was what made him laugh the most- but he still played his part. He had lived his life in the lap of luxury; how drastically things had changed.

We had all taken space from each other, in our quarters or in the command room, although Orthopox stayed in the kitchen and laughed at the behavior of a friendly cricket. Abdi thought it was funny that he had drunk three bottles of wine and was going to get a fourth. Finally, once the gas wore off, Jamie stood up from her captain's chair and picked up the microphone to the ship's intercom.

"If you thought that was funny, go to the recreational room and play some clips from Earth's finest comedians!" announced Jamie jokingly to the exhaustedly unenthusiastic response of the crew.

"All funny business aside, if you would like to avoid this happening again, please practice showing social skills that are conducive to a crew worthy of being called, The Cosmic Liberation Alliance. Yes, that's right, I had time to think of a name for our crew during your laughing gas trips! Please see your way to your quarters, if you aren't already there, and reflect on the briefing we had during a dinner that will not soon be forgotten. Save your questions for The Rebel Atlantean and do not leave your rooms until we make our destination," commanded the captain.

CHAPTER 20

Venessa, Orthopox, Sid, Muhammad, Abdi, Captain Jamie Southerns, and I finally felt the spaceship touch the surface of Svetlana. We strategically and discreetly parked outside the safe house and made our way inside. We accomplished all this with eerily easy stealth and agility that we used to not be detected, which we were quite proud of. Svetlana was currently under siege by the Komodians who were under orders to arrest any of us if we were found, though they weren't looking hard on the planet they likely assumed we had all fled.

The plan was to convene in a place that was in plain sight but inconspicuous enough to where we wouldn't be discovered. We didn't think the Komodians would think to look under their noses for us. The Ancient Rebel Atlantean met us as soon as we entered the downward elevator doors. Myself and the party I was with felt that we were in the presence of royalty. Not only that, we were being met by someone legendary but humble enough to be the one to greet us. Sid reached out with his bourgeoise attire and mannerisms and kissed her hand.

The doors to the elevator opened and The Rebel kindly asked Rasumetan, who was a rather uncouth but obviously extremely educated human being, to be our guide and apologized that she could not stay longer. On the way to showing us to our rooms, he said he was a philosophy expert. Unlike attendants who accepted their position as staff hired to take care of the facility who did not engage with members of the Council (as their higher status meant that they had more wealth and better things to think about), he seemed confident in his thinking prowess, but not in a way that overstepped his boundaries. Rasumetan engaged with us by asking questions and telling us about himself, as well as what type of opinions he valued. The tour comprised the seemingly endless halls, with rooms that had been carved out of the mountain and turned into a safe house.

Rasumetan asked us questions and, like most highly educated people do, made inquiries about the political correctness that surrounded each subject we talked about. Correctness, which did in fact exist in the sense that preconceived notions and assumptions about our social reality exist in our minds as social constructs; i.e. psychological constructs that exist in our thought processes but are not clear in the material world.

"I take an approach to social interaction, and that approach leans towards how I can help and drives me to wonder about my own assumptions. I have often been of the opinion that we become so absolved inside our problems that it passes our mind to ask questions about life or think what a gift life is to begin with. But if you would rather me quiet down, there is no sense in me speaking to people who don't want to listen," inquired Rasumetan nonchalantly.

"I have been a Queen of an entire colony of people called the Norvegicans. Yet there are many other leaders on my planet who take different approaches, and some of whom have even more political sway than myself. You don't think I became a Queen without thinking about political correctness, do you? No, please, speak whenever you wish, but don't feel pressured to do so. Say the best things that come to your mind because we are already on the same side," said Nubia warmly and with admiration of having a person with some experience in philosophy.

"Keep in mind, young man, that I do not subscribe to the idea of mental illness- I think that although illness of the mind exists, that phrase is often used so that the social picture is run like a military academy. I for one would rather you converse over any topic you wish, and I expect that grace returned. And if I grow tired, I will take leave, but in most circumstances, I am all ears for anyone with an acute sense of observation and who pays close attention to the matters at hand- not just being smart in their thoughts but applying their intelligence to what is happening circumstantially," the Queen said with a solemn sense of directness.

"Yes ma'am, I mean, yes Queen Nubia, that is crystal clear. Thank you for giving me this opportunity! Am I part of your team now?" asked the philosophically inclined Rasumetan.

Queen Nubia looked up as her mouse-shaped body only went up to Rasumetan's waistline. "I have a good feeling about you, Rasumetan. My character judgment is faster and more accurate than most. So yes, since you have nothing better to do than give tours to people, you may now call yourself a member of the Cosmic Liberation Alliance. That is the name of our team you will soon be introduced to," expressed Nubia, who was overjoyed to have another person help with the mission at hand.

"We will reconvene in an hour. Talk to council members in the meantime and ask them questions you think are relevant. We will answer the other gaps in our understanding of how to make this relationship functional as we progress. As of right now, we are skimp for time, and I must take a brief nap before the council meeting takes place," said the Queen as she politely stood in her doorway preparing to close the door.

"As may not be customary to say, but I feel an existential excitement towards being alive and am happy to have the support of someone who I know will listen to me after a long day of talking to people and expressing my altruistic personality. After all, I believe the meaning of life is to talk about meaningful things," mentioned Rasumetan, who was prepared to follow the Queen's directions wherever it led.

"Yes, and remember these people aren't the most trustful bunch. In fact, I would not put it past half of them to get into an argument over the price of rice in China five minutes into the start of the conference. Although I have great faith in the lead speaker tonight, the representative from the planet Atlantis; who knows... perhaps you will be the speaker another night. Thank you Rasumetan," whispered Queen Nubia as she gently locked the door.

CHAPTER 21

She was tall and practically skin and bones. Her large round head and lack of nostrils stressed her pale brown skin and large black eyes. The Atlantean wore a simple mossy green sash that covered her breasts and lower extremities.

"I'm delighted to find you all together and safe. This tragic series of events leading up to a political arrest was not something I ever thought would actually happen. But now that you all are here, allow me to help you all get settled before we discuss tactics. I will be happy to answer your questions. I must admit, as an individual capable of reasoning about the decisions I plan to make with a wise mind, my mind has been apprehensive about being here today.

"At least, that is the advice given to me by the High Order of Oracles on my home planet. I went against their advice by being with you today per the verdict that the Atlanteans should not meddle in business that isn't our own. I have to say that I have hope in a successful outcome in this war which is yet to be officially declared. I am also aware of this portion of the Orion Arm Council of Peace having filed a grievance with this regions Universal Jury. It is my opinion that this decision is appropriate; however, today I bring with me new information to share with you all.

"As you prepare for the council's meeting tonight where I will be the lead speaker, is that anyone we give the vaccine to (which I also helped develop) will be at no risk of being reinfected with the Millennial 2084 virus or any of its variants. The vaccine is safe, and the more vaccines we deliver, the safer and more probable our success in this mission will be. Our chief aim is to vaccinate everyone in the Orion Arm and yes- the vaccination will also work on people who have already been exposed to Millennial 2084 and its oral counterpart Soma," said The Ancient.

"Also, something else to keep in mind is that this new information I am sharing is intended to shed light on the vast amount of uncertainty that has taken place since the political divide within the council. Specifically, dear friends, my aim is to reunite the council by revealing the motives behind the man who has risen to the highest branches of power in this sector. I urge each of you to keep an open mind and try and understand the bridges I have and continue to create. The reason I've felt compelled to go against the advice of the leadership on my planet is because of the potential life in the Orion Arm has in the future destiny of the totality of life in the Milky Way and beyond," said The Rebel.

This person known as The Rebel who had previously announced that her home planet was called Atlantis then dismissed the mandatory preliminary meeting to dinner. As for herself, she took an offer from our very own Muhammad.

The ice was broken when, while everyone else was storming to the buffet line, Muhammad went the other direction and confronted the Rebel with the following interaction. "Excuse me ma'am, but may I be so meek as to inquire where I might find another woman as bold and as beautiful as you? I only ask after seeing how fearlessly you're tackling this political nightmare; I can only assume that either you have a very special someone you like, have a spouse, or you are a lesbian!"

The Ancient, who was now being called an Atlantean by the groups sitting at tables and eating, was charmed by Muhammad's lightheartedness and accepted an invitation to sit at their table along with Abdi. The president of the council, who went by the name of Vevo, shortly after asked if he could join their table, taking one of the empty seats. After becoming acquainted with the people at her table, especially Muhammad who could make the Rebel laugh like a charm, it was not long after that Queen Nubia had finished eating and started the trend of walking up to the presidents table and giving an introduction.

CHAPTER 22

"Hey Arnold, do you want to spend the night together? I mean… I already know we're sharing the same room, but do you think we could have some personal time with each other and really connect with our feelings?" Zeke asked as I was drying off with a towel after a hot shower.

My stomach was filled with butterflies at Zeke's sincere desire to hang out together and connect on a personal level. I was happy that we could be so open together. So, what I did next was take off the towel and walk buck naked right over to him and sit on his lap.

I looked into his dazzling blue eyes, and it was only after feeling our souls connected and meshed together that he leaned in and kissed me. We continued twirling our tongues around together and pretty soon, both of us had climaxed.

As we cuddled in the bed on his side of the room, catching our breath, Zeke surprised me with yet another offer.

"I know we are attending a council meeting tonight, during which you will have to explain how your ex-boyfriend died. I know this will not be easy, but I think if you chime in at a good time- the odds of them understanding who I am and why human life is also capable of much more than war will help make it clear where humanity stands in this fight," Zeke sought to ease my emotional pain at the mentioning of Samuel.

"Well, the job of the council is to establish peace. Now that our mission will be to vaccinate entire planets, we're going to face the greater problem of how to go about making peace without taking away free will. We are going to the conference together, but they are still preparing to make the official announcement that Jamie will be the second senator for Earth in replacement of Samuel Yellowstone. Yet, Nubia and Sid also suggested the possibility that the three of us confer amongst ourselves and take turns speaking since we are so new; it is still to be decided."

x

We got dressed in formal attire and made our way to the new council chamber. On our way there, we met with Jamie, Sid, and Queen Nubia. Entering the conference room, which was a small stadium-like room with a semi-wrap-around-stage, except instead of theater seats, there were tables which were in place so that the council members could have discussions and so that they would have a place to write down questions they would like to pose to the speaker.

Muhammad and Abdi had been invited to sit with their species, but the rest of our crew, including Venessa, sat at our own designated table. It was at our table that we re-encountered Rasumetan who had busied himself volunteering with a job being a waiter serving concessions, which turned out rather profitable for him in how he accumulated quite a few tips- each more than twice what I had made working for the university newspaper.

Rasumetan asked us if we wanted any refreshments and told us what he had learned since we last saw him, speaking mainly to Queen Nubia. Then, once the crowded council chamber calmed, Rasumetan took his invitation to sit next to Zeke, Jamie, and me. We were the only four humans in the room out of eighty-six life-forms. The rest of the council members either could not make it or couldn't be trusted not to expose our location to the Svetlanian Gestapo, who the Komodians had forced into doing their bidding for risk of being controlled as well.

Moments passed by after roll was called and everyone who was scheduled to be present was accounted for. Moments in time that to most of the people in the make-shift council chamber passed with an uneasy feeling of anxiety.

It was Gilgamesh who announced the Atlantean who went by the alias of The Rebel onto the stage.

"It is with great pleasure and extreme honor that I introduce the woman who has been the talk of the last few nights, the person who we all hope will put an end to the great civil unrest and mental anguish we've all been through…" Gilgamesh glanced over at The Ancient who signaled for him to proceed.

"But before I hand over the microphone, allow me to leave you with a bit of humor…" He paused and drank down a shot of Folivorian Whiskey. The audience prepared for the humor that was about to be conveyed through the Norvegican.

"On Earth, there is a species of non-sentient life that looks similar to the people on my planet. They are called mice! Of course, unless you go into the sewers of New York City, the Norvegicans are much larger and we walk on two feet- we've been compared to the size of Yoda from Star Wars, albeit furrier, and with rounded noses!"

This line got a slight comical reaction from the audience.

"Well, as chance would have it, the Norvegicans have a natural predator on our home planet Regus called… FLEAS!"

Again, the audience laughed at the sarcasm.

"So now that we have cured our flea problem, we would one day like to welcome you all to our planet where you find that, unlike the mouse population on Earth, the Norvegicans are not afraid of cats!" This created a round of thunder to which Gilgamesh, who had put on a suit and tie for a change, took a bow and made way for The Atlantean Rebel to take the stage.

She was lanky, still wearing the simple mossy green sash over her breasts and covering her lower extremities. Her face was still young despite her advanced age, full of life, and one could tell her heart was filled with goodwill from her facial expressions.

"There is nothing worse than someone asking for help and not getting it," started The Atlantean, thus changing the ambiance in the room.

CHAPTER 23

The Rebel's elegant body motions and her soft but precise enunciation of her words captivated our attention.

"First, let me explain why they call me The Rebel. My home planet of Atlantis comprises a race of people that once, at least two hundred thousand years ago- not to mention my age- occupied this arm of the galaxy. We governed your civilizations until a political movement swept over our minds dealing with our feelings that your races should develop on their own, free of our intervention; which is why we left the Orion Arm.

"To be frank, this was primarily because we advanced technologically as we discovered how to sail across the vast emptiness of space and arrive at other galaxies. During that time, Atlantis, with my help, invented a pathogen we experimented with that would be used in the same manner it has been used here- to end wars and stop criminals from violating the rights of other sentient life. We simply got tired of seeing so much violence occurring. We got tired of destroying civilization and seeing it rebuild itself only to fall into the same path of destruction. This is why the Oracles found it within reason to hinder your future advancement by employing the use of this pathogen.

"Yet, after seeing how ineffective it was in that it caused the decay of evolutionary advancement, we could not ethically allow such a policy to stay in place. I, along with many other gifted scientists, then created a cure which we shared with you on December 24th. Still, this intervention was not effective either because the use of it was quickly outlawed by this Orion Council majority, though not present at this time, who claimed the Millennial 2084 pathogen would continue to be used until a better solution was found."

"We thought we had distributed the antiviral cure to every planet that had been infected until the Armodafians discovered the planet Plecostomus, which contained a species that had regressed in an evolutionary point of view so much so that their very neurons were beginning to decompose to the extent that their brains, which were once humanoid, could no longer function.

"At one point we even used the virus on our own people who were thought to be a detriment to the sanctuary-like atmosphere that our society and educational system thrived to achieve. I took a lead stance against such measures and put my scientifically inclined mind to work on developing a vaccination. It was thought that the Planet Plecostomus could never be discovered by any life in the Orion Arm. After seeing the decomposition of the cognitive and physical stability of the Plecostomusian people, the High Order of Oracles accepted that the virus could no longer be used as a means to cure people who were called hazards of armistice; and I use this word because like every other planet we have observed, we ourselves had wars amongst ourselves. It was because the last great war practically wiped out our entire race we originally started looking for a way to deactivate the brain's ability to respond to its environment with aggressive behavior.

"Almost all the Atlanteans took the vaccine because it was thought that our species would more likely survive war than it would decaying into organisms that would without a doubt go extinct due to the decomposition of neuronal tissue. Therefore, much like your species is now learning, ending the disorganization caused by our more destructive instinct had to be solved by other means. It really is a miracle that we have survived this long, as civil unrest occurred many times after the abandonment of these policy solutions. I became known as The Rebel, not because I didn't want what everyone else did, but because I led the team that discovered the cure that without would have surely meant our demise," spoke The Rebel.

The room was filled with attentive ears who had already heard this much of the story but were relieved to have heard the truth from a reliable source. Zeke took my hand, which was sweaty, and said he felt like something was terribly wrong. The Rebel glanced over at us as if hearing him and continued.

"... pretty soon Lord Komodo will discover our location, but do not be alarmed- this is all according to plans. You see, I have come to know Komodo, and we have worked together to see that a solution could be enacted at the opportune moment that would enable to council to reunite. Komodo has secretly been part of the council minority all along, but together we are bringing the entire council together to witness an event that will quite possibly solve this dilemma," The Rebel stated with as much encouragement as she could.

Suddenly, the alarm systems blared and the emergency lights came on, causing anxieties to rise.

"I saw no other way to convince the people of Atlantis that it is possible for us to share our technology and work together. This plan was set into motion because of my heartfelt belief and hope in universal peace." Her words were pronounced more quickly. "Lord Komodo is still part of this council, is he not?"

A murmur of disquiet and suspicion clamored across the chamber. Not long after that, Komodo's team of secret police entered the chamber, whereby they locked all of us in and, one by one placed us in electronic cuffs as a precautionary measure.

"Ah, here he comes now. Let us welcome our once highly thought of senator and keeper of the peace. Let us give him the same opportunity to show his humanity as someone who is just as imperfect and flawed as the people of my planet and each of you in this room..." The Rebel advised as the microphone was taken away and she was placed into special custody with the technology on her wrist was taken away.

"CLEAR!" said a boisterous voice, signaling to Komodo that the coast was clear for him to make his appearance.

"I heard every word of your speech, Rebel Atlantean, which is why I am offering two solutions," announced Lord Komodo. "The first option is that you all agree to comply with the status of this mission. Travel with me to Atlantis using this technology," offered Komodo as he held up the transportation device that had been given to him.

Komodo hesitated briefly to gather his thoughts and continued with more gusto than before, "Second, you can choose to take the less appealing approach and wait here in custody until I return in being victorious in allocating the means to liberate the tribes of sentient life gathered here today in this chamber. The latter option is less risky, but it brings with it the possibility that once I gather the technology, I use it for my own personal gain and do not share. Keep in mind that outside this haven you've created in this expired coal mine, the rest of the council are in orbit above this planet called Svetlana. Together, we can negotiate with these beings and use their technology to establish peace," said Komodo.

The Atlantean took up the microphone and clarified that her race would likely be willing to share a small portion of their technological achievements if she were to be brought in as a hostage.

"And just how do you expect that achieving intergalactic travel would create peace?" demanded Queen Nubia, asking the most obvious question. "Did it every occur to you that even if we spread across the universe, these same delinquents that you've been attempting to fix will eventually gain the same technology you hope to achieve through these negotiations?"

Lord Komodo cleared his throat as the thought of intergalactic war made him overcome with trepidation. "I believe that peace cannot be achieved unless we work together. What is certain is that statistical analysis shows that poverty is the primary cause of crimes against the peace. Having advanced travel will allow those less fortunate more opportunities to achieve a better life and access to better information. With that, I realize there are issues, but it is a solution that I feel qualifies as 'until we find something better', and therefore the virus no longer has to be a temporary solution. If I am successful, this council must agree to its own terms and end the use of the Millennial 2084 pathogen. That way the System of Correction can be dissolved and I can step down and simply help my people once more.

"This is my suggestion, you may take it or leave it, but I declare that a vote take place immediately," added Komodo.

Many of the council members were still trying to wrap their heads around the fact that Komodo did not desire to be a tyrant. Instead, he was doing exactly what he thought was best for life in the Orion Arm. Zeke, who was now my boyfriend, raised his hands courageously in order to ask a question.

After being ignored by bickering senators, he loudly announced that he wanted to ask a question and the entire chamber looked over at us. Following this, Komodo gestured for him to say what was on his mind. "Will we have time to discuss this issue civilly or will it be rushed through?" Zeke asked with an air of mastery over the situation.

Lord Komodo spoke to his communicator for the rest of the members to join us in the makeshift council chamber. Pretty soon the room was filled with all 152 council members, and those in cuffs were released from physical confinement, including The Rebel Atlantean. What amounted after that was a discussion that lasted six hours. At the end of the sixth hour, a vote was cast and the vast majority of the council agreed to go ahead with Komodo's plan to go to Atlantis.

The Rebel, having already explained that the technology she wore around her wrist would not be enough to take everyone and that she did not have the exact specification of how the technology functioned, agreed to take a small group of senators along with her and Komodo to her home planet of Atlantis.

Having been the one to ask about the vote, Zeke was elected to go with The Rebel and his request to bring me and Jamie was accepted. Before we left, Venessa approached her once spiritual guru with more attitude toward having left her in Muhammad's house to die in a fire. The two of them apologized to each other after a long and extremely heated discussion and, for reasons I was never sure of, they parted with a kiss on the lips.

CHAPTER 24

Komodo, Zeke, Jamie and I gathered in front of The Rebel, who had opened a portal to her planet. Once the portal was opened, she was placed in handcuffs and made to look like a hostage. We walked through and found ourselves present on a long walkway that led to a group of Ancients sitting on large stone chairs in a semicircle. As we all walked forward, prepared to face our biggest challenge yet, Komodo led the way and the four of us followed behind. It was strange to be teaming up with this person we had thought of for so long as our enemy. But we had agreed to give him the benefit of the doubt. We agreed to trust that he wanted what was best for the galaxy, especially his own people.

The portal shut behind us and as we approached the semicircle of Ancients who were prepared to talk with us about whatever it was that we wanted. This was so that they could ensure the safety of one of their own citizens, which to them was a top priority.

There were six Oracles who immediately release The Rebel from cuffs and instructed to take her place as the seventh. Apparently, The Rebel had not anticipated her counterparts catching onto her plan so quickly. Until that point, we did not know The Rebel an Oracle. The other Oracles glanced at her with different expressions- one with disgust and another with an expression of anxiety. The Ancient Atlantean in the center wore a hoity-toity robe. Remarkable how distinguished each of the personalities of the seven Oracles was.

"We come here today as representatives from life in the

Orion Arm. We come in peace and would like to negotiate for permission to have access to your technology," Komodo declared. Having been put in an awkward situation, the Oracle in the center spoke first, calm but stern. Of course, the Oracles knew everything about Komodo and also could read his mind. Yet, Komodo was intelligent enough to keep up and was never once placed in a pigeonhole that he couldn't get out of; equating to the fact that, if necessary, he actually would kill The Atlanteans, something that The Rebel had known all along. They prodded him for some time about his behavior concerning the virus and conquering a multitude of planets, which he answered that he was honestly prepared to distribute the vaccination and release his prisoners from psychological bondage if they would hand over the technology he desired.

After some time, the center Oracle spoke, "We agree to help, primarily because we do not feel that you will ever have the ability to become a threat to us. First, we will finish the job we should have done ourselves to begin with- vaccinating the Orion Arm against the free will incapacitating virus; we will also help you with this. Second, you may have access to our intergalactic travel technology. You will now have the blueprints of the technology on your spaceships and will find it already capable of intergalactic travel."

I was never sure how they acted so quickly, but not long after that, dozens of ships from the Orion Arm appeared in orbit around Atlantis.

"We have much to learn from each other, and by working as a team and developing friendships, we will work together for the common good of all races in this galaxy and others that we have found," said the female Oracle who went by the name of Kubica.

"Let us part in peace and aspire to continue keeping peace by working together to solve social issues," said the Oracle in the center who introduced himself as Hammurabi.

With the help of the new technology, vaccinations, which also acted as a cure to those already infected, quickly got delivered to each of the planets the council members came from, starting with those that had been infected. We agreed that any new planet that was visited, including Plecostomus, would automatically volunteer the vaccination to be received to protect from any future threats.

x

Keep in mind that there was a reason Lord Komodo had so skillfully been able to not only have the knowledge about where the council members of the antiviral party were meeting, but he also able to almost effortlessly achieve his mission to sway them into working together. That reason was that Komodo and The Rebel had been meeting in secret.

Originally, she contacted him during the time she was in this sector of the galaxy, between the time Jamie and Thaddeus had sent thier message and awaited a response from the Atlanteans using the gifted intellect of Ramos Destin Uphanivan. Her intent was to inform him of her plans to vaccinate the entire galaxy.

After talking with The Rebel, she learned of how the council could use the information she provided against him as a way of claiming that he was attempting to start a rebellion. Not wanting to appear insubordinate, The Rebel Atlantean watched him from afar as he struggled more and more about using the virus to enslave worlds. When she saw his feelings were genuine, she decided to see if she could work with him to sow the seeds of discord among the council and make the group split- which is exactly what happened over time, leading up to a fraction of the council taking refuge in the renovated coal mines of Svetlana.

Komodo continued to enslave the civilizations of insubordinate planets per the orders of the council. Simultaneously,

The Rebel worked to contact the appointed senators of each infected world. They saw this plan to usurp the groupthink of the council majority as the only way to stop the very thing they were perpetuating.

The process of dividing the council even further than when the original vote on the matter took place took time. Originally, Komodo only agreed with The Rebel's plan because of the future prospect of having a more peaceful network of planets than could ever be achieved with the council's current policies and procedures. This prospect was held in place via the potential opportunities that The Rebel opened up for Komodo.

Komodo's plan was to obtain technology that would enable intergalactic travel brought upon by the gamut of technological advancements The Rebel could provide by her social opening into the Atlantean circle. This meant other ways of handling criminal disciplinary action would become probable.

Of course, this did not go on without the most despised and revered dictator experiencing a large amount of anxiety. Namely because his actions in this matter made him out to be a criminal in how he secretly disobeyed the direct orders of the council, as well as how he was not honest in doing the job his salary assigned him. At least, that is how the amoral council majority would interpret his behavior.

Not only did Komodo feel anxiety over his noncompliance with the standards he agreed to follow, but also, he felt like a deplorable person. Someone who had traded his value system and sense of morality so that he could lift his species out of poverty at the cost of others.

The Komodians, whose species proper name of reference is Reperoritian, were a peaceful race. Their spiritual leaders taught that a higher power could be found through their struggle and with their destitute lifestyle; they taught it was through a symbiosis with the planet and with each other that their prosperity would grow.

Yet, Komodo had brought an exorbitant amount of wealth to their planet which corrupted the men and caused the women to turn from their prudent way of life. This caused the spiritual leaders to experience great distress. On many occasions, they attempted to reason with their former pupil, and this tore Komodo psychologically. This was because Komodo had never intended his race to become a nefariously abased group of degenerates.

What ended up happening was that certain people of Reperoritas bribed and exploited Komodo. This was primarily because the spiritual leaders had refused to communicate with him after many attempts to reason, and so he was forced to find other sources of company. The fact of the matter was that Komodo was not willing to put his people back into poverty. It was not known by many, but more than often whenever he could find a spare moment to be alone, Komodo would feel as if he were a personal example of a disgrace. A shameful person who had caused even more disorder and who propagated heathenism both on his home world as well as on the planets he spread the virus on.

In fact, the council never approved of an official religion to convert the mind slaves to. Truth be told, the original monuments erected in Komodo's image were not funded by this very misunderstood dictator. Yet once a religion began to form around him, the council observed how obedience was commanded in his name, and this was something they approved of. They thought this was understandable because allegedly they were dealing with criminals, though in reality this was largely a pronounced error in judgment. Lack of understanding or education led to criminalization.

There were many times Komodo wanted to destroy these shrines. Yet, the council majority, who he met with often, strongly discouraged this as (in the name of "peace" which became a world that in most instances equated to an act of oppression) doing so would disrupt the routine of the mind slaves.

Once Komodo even walked the streets of Manhattan dressed in discrete clothing, making him indiscernible to the untrained eye. He observed how humanity had lost its spirit. He lamented how the human race who once was abundant in individuality and encompassed a wide diversity of cultural personalities no longer had any resemblance of a society with any type of uniqueness.

He even went so far as to, while eating at Taco Bueno, walk up to an ordinary citizen, a twenty-something year old man and confront him.

"Sir, may I intrude for a moment and ask a question that has been on my mind for some time now?" questioned Komodo.

"Certainly. But sir, I must point out that you have mistakenly not dressed in the appropriate uniform that is needed to be successful in today's social procedures. We are celebrating the world being free of idiosyncrasies. We no longer have to be self-conscious about our way of thinking because we now follow the handbook of social protocol," the man laughed before Komodo could correct him. "Allow me to offer you a spare uniform that I have in my automobile. I just paid to have it repainted to the socially correct color, which was fine because I traded in all of my guns and signed a document saying that I would abide by the new constitution. I'll be right back- let me go retrieve the proper uniform or else I will be forced to report you!"

"Shut up you fool!" shouted Komodo angrily. "Do you really find any meaning following these social obligations day in and day out. Being that you've been stricken by a disease that was purposefully brought about by an alien race you've never heard of... Being that you are mindlessly following any directions you are told... Don't you ever feel like fighting back?"

Komodo shook the man violently and shouted, "Well do you!"

Everyone in Taco Bell glared ignorantly at the scene.

"Don't you remember what it was like to do things on your own free will? To start each day fresh and free of any kind of socially dictated behavioral dance that you do every day? Can't you just please show me what it was like for you all before the virus happened? The council ruled to contaminate this planet with the Millennial 2084 pathogen before we even genuinely had the chance to see how beautiful the human race was... Don't you see! WE MADE A MISTAKE!" cried Komodo in a desperate plea to see an ounce of humanity left in this person's soul.

When Komodo looked into the young man's eyes all he saw was a blank stare. He had been stripped of every glimmer of humanity. Suddenly, security people dressed in official uniforms stormed in with heavy duty artillery and bullet proof shields.

"Stop in the name of the Orion Arm Security Force." A man plunged a tool at Komodo's arm which took his blood. Shortly after the security agent announced, "The Millennial 2084 is not in his system! Call headquarters!"

As soon as the agent made this announcement, Komodo pulled out a smoke grenade. He threw it towards the security guards and a white mist quickly filled the room. The mist was also filled with the vaccination which ended the psychological enslavement temporarily.

He continued shooting people with the temporary antidote until his path was clear and he could make it back into his shuttlecraft. But before he left this city devoid of human spirit and individual personalities, he went back over to the man who he had been speaking with rather impolitely.

"You sons of bitches! You've taken everything from us!" screamed the twenty-something year old man. Just as the temporary antidote was wearing off, Komodo removed the man's hands that had been strangling him and he scurried off, quickly returning to his spaceship in a matter of minutes.

CHAPTER 25

This part of the story ends back on my home planet Earth. The vaccinations were given to each person through soda pops. The soda pops were filled with the antiviral serum which, once consumed, set into motion the adverse effects of the Millennial 2084 virus. Billions of these drinks were made and it was sufficiently safe to drink more than one of them. Even infants were given the baby soda pop, and seeing their eyes look around at the world for what was consciously the first time was an experience I would never forget with my son Alward.

In a matter of days, any of the few remaining Space Rangers were chased off the planet. This was done because humans stormed the arsenals and took control of military equipment, even those belonging to the Reperoritian. Humanity had become aware of the freedom that they had regained, and in no possible scenario were they prepared to lose it again. In fact, a great psychological liberation took place on a global scale that was unlike any cognitive awakening in human history. All the leaders of each country were apprised about what had taken place and measures were taken to ensure that Earth's psychological freedom would forever be safe.

Once things cooled off, Zeke and I went back to my parent's house and were introduced to my son, who Samantha had named Alward Brady Fitzgerald. Not long after- perhaps a month of living in the awkward situation of having a boyfriend and also a wife- Samantha and I agreed we could not remain a couple and so we filed for divorce. About a year later she was seen during my wedding to Zeke with her new fiancé Terry Raymore, whom everyone called Tank.

Samuel Yellowstone's body was recovered from the morgue on Malcolm's ship. We gave him a proper burial and were able to say our last words during his funeral. My union to Zeke was performed alongside the union of Sid and Jamie, as well as the union of Komodo and Venessa. It was a Christian service and over two thousand people attended from many planets. Zeke and I loved each other and still cared for my son, who would not long after have the last name of Raymore.

I finished my education in political science and eventually became a diplomat like Sid. Zeke became a captain of an intergalactic starship, whereby he kept his promise to King Thaddeus to help spread peace and prosperity in galaxies all over the universe. King Thaddeus' planet of Polunin was rebuilt, and the population continues to spike upwards in a new era of peace and prosperity.

As for Malcolm, she would eventually have to answer for her behavior. Still not sure of how to rehabilitate criminals, she was sent to an oasis planet where she would live by herself and never interfere with council matters again. Each infected planet became free from the virus with which they had been controlled by people who thought freedom could not exist unless it was commanded.

There was an old chubby Palorian man with a long beard and mustache who was a member of the council who proclaimed during the original meeting to decide if a vote should be cast or not, "Man can only be free if he is imprisoned in some capacity, otherwise he will not act morally."

Yet once the council listened to the advice of The Rebel Atlantean and began the vaccination, a new discussion about the meaning of liberty resulted. Of course, Komodo had only gone to Planet Atlantis to speak to the Oracles about obtaining the technology he requested. This was granted to him and every planet with intelligent life within the Orion Arm of the Milky Way was welcomed into the Galactic Coalition.

Before Komodo, Zeke, Jamie, and I left Atlantis, the entire council including all one hundred and fifty-two senators was invited into the ballroom which was located at the top of a large skyscraper. Our group listened to the wisdom of the Oracles who stated that the galaxy is not going to exist in a perfect state of peace. We must work on building bridges and healthy relationships and have hope in our efforts to search for new ways of establishing peace. By doing this, grudges that have been held long and hard feelings kept locked deep inside will heal and progress towards a peaceful universe that can continue to advance.

THE END

A friend is today, tomorrow is a bonus. -Mark Hammond Baker

Hi, fellow sentient life-forms! I originally conceived this series during the start of the pandemic. It was read while socially distancing and self-isolating due to COVID-19. I had tons of fun writing these two quick and easy reads! I expect you appreciated this second novel in the "Shackles of Conformity Series." This next section of this book is the introduction to a future novel that I will write with the ambition to publish. As of right now, I have a third book in this series already in the works. Be that as it may, I am currently writing a standalone novel about

Neanderthal people that will be released prior to the next book in this series.

The figure "King Thaddeus" in this short story that I may continue into a novel its introduction. Undoubtedly taken from the character of the series you've just read, however, this time, I've organized the role of King Thaddeus into a human personality. I made this decision because his spirit enamored me, and I wanted to discover what it would be like if he were a real person instead of a jellyfish-like alien. Please let me know what you think! You can email your opinions and points of view on anything you've read of mine at the following address: baker3mh@gmail.com. Thank you for reading!

Bonus Content!

Title: Nuclear Holocaust

Written By: Mark Hammond Baker

October 9, 2021

My name is Thaddeus. At least that is the appellation I go by since my discovery of a highly curious assortment of records. To be frank, at one point, I was a monarch. Though because of what I now announce as the beliefs of the Second Civilization, they robbed me of my crown- dethroned by my brethren.

The answers are not absolutely apparent. What precipitated the downfall of the First Civilization has afflicted my mind for the grander part of a decade. My visions have driven me to contemplate an array of convictions.

Before reading these records secretly for years along with my partner of whom, upon them witnessing our bodies intertwined, made my brethren perform the sacred ritual that rid me of my divinity and manifested my mortality. They threw me into the dungeon along with mere mortals who had been deposited there by my very orders. People who can now be part of the intellectual awakening that I and my compatriot will soon set into motion. Even though I once considered them criminals because they refused to worship me, these insurgents refused to believe in the theology of our time; one that had coincidentally placed me on the pedestal. Though in my defense, I was as much a slave to the religion as those who prayed to me.

Oh, how many religions must have defined humanity over the millennia! As there are merely ten thousand years of recorded history that exist in the Second Civilization and that our contemporary ideologies have not shifted in all this time, it is now unmistakable that alternative means of spirituality have dwelt before what we have determined to be the creation of our race.

In our Second Civilization, during the time I was king, I had proved myself as an admirable and exalted divine individual. We currently have beliefs that now, because of the venerable text we discovered, have all been placed into dispute.

My brethren, I must explain that I have studied this dialect, and from it I have learned of events that arose or perhaps did not literally take place during the First Civilization. The revelation of the Holy Scriptures, if we resolve to go on calling them by this name during this day of human survival, was carried out through an excavation through which a forty-thousand-year-old time capsule was located, much older than our known history.

My purpose in writing this, as a leader who cares profoundly about the type of world we construct as our civilization progresses, is to convey how crucial it is to take precautions so that this genius plan is not turned against us. That is why I am informing you all that this book was unearthed. That these ancient writings bear with it the ability (as I have experienced) to arouse the soul to an extent. Though it may simply have been the fascination with my discovery, the anticipation of what I could achieve with this learning and the cognitive maturity involving intellectual liberation that followed through my understanding of a society that existed without God destroying it as deserved by not observing the rituals accordingly led me to ponder more.

I remain to question if our understanding of a celestial being who malevolently destroyed the realm was not in fact done instead by our very hands. I contend that the First Civilization, as indisputable in the technology seen in the time capsule, developed technology that we have not achieved. It is likely that humans destroyed themselves, not God. I substantiate this with how direct God's pledge to Noah was in the Old Testament that he would never again destroy humankind; though perhaps he did so in other ways.

I was king when the time capsule was appropriated, and I took it upon myself to keep the book for myself; by some miracle it had survived, while nothing but dust and old wreckage remained of the other objects left inside. I deciphered and interpreted this extraordinarily dated book, which according to the date written on the capsule was forty thousand years ago. Then, after being caught in what was said to be a debaucherously heinous iniquity, I suffered my exile and dethronement from my kinghood. Yet my male companion (the source of my disgrace), who means more to me than any friend ever could, studied these scriptures along with me over the past decade.

What is most striking about this discovery is the contrasts and sameness between the culture of the lives that currently dwell in this realm and those that I argue read this book as an authority of spiritual direction. It may be of tremendous profit to know more about who I am, how I have dreamed about this discovery, and what I plan to do with this newfound wisdom.

I'll start by recounting how I became the famous monarch of the entirety of contemporary civilization. Everyone below the heavens looked up to me as a ruler, yet I failed in my duty to coordinate my personal opinions with the long-held religious doctrines of our world. This was because I clung to the old beliefs, which I now more than ever realize poison our mental disposition to grow intellectually.

It is obvious to me now that I only instilled the theological beliefs of our time into our peoples because that is how the forefathers of the crown had preserved order and demanded obedience. Duplicating the information in this book discovered in the time capsule and distributing it around the seven provinces will generate complications (hopefully a revolution), but I will do whatever it takes to show the peoples of this realm that Tobias and I are together its rightful rulers.

The new found knowledge carries with it the idea that in history, quite before this kingdom had been formed by our divine creator, there was another human civilization that existed that was politically organized in ways our doctrine would condemn anyone of heresy were they to mention it. Of course, our present and long-held beliefs rest on the perception that noble blood was not born of flesh, but was rather placed here by the almighty being who instilled the authority to govern man within them. Yet, the discovery of the Bible may change that. All evidence of the First Civilization would all be but forbidden rumors of lost or indiscernible ancient architecture. What modern superstition could not explain were it not for religious dogma. Yet it is now clear that there are ancient architectural structures predating our own trust in when life began, and it is explained by life on this planet having existed before the oldest of our records. The only foundation I have to base my theory of the existence of a First Civilization predating this one is that there is no evidence of a book or language like this ever being found.

Regardless of the technicalities or conflict in the strength of our philosophical argument, we will still unite as followers of Christ Jesus! If it be not only for the simple sake of experiencing psychological autonomy from those who have exploited us into thinking, we can have no separate opinion than that which is called for by the nobility currently in power. My faith in Jesus still staggers, but I plan on using these texts against those who have not only stolen my throne, but who will be exposed for attempting to make a buffoonery out of the citizenry! We will do so by killing the king- thus proving he is mortal!

I follow this by saying that this language I am writing in, which took the larger part of an entire decade to learn, has never been seen before. Finally, the most considerable evidence for there being a preceding civilization, if not more, is the manner in which I found the book of what they once called the Holy Bible.

The characters described in this artifact, which predates the oldest of dates ever before predicted to be the date of creation, may have been real or they may have been an assemblage of fantasy; though I trust that there is still plenty to be learned from this discovery. What is notable is the passion aroused in my spirit upon reading about the all too relatable struggles that these prehistoric (and likely unevolved) people encountered.

Our sense of God is denounced by these texts. Our society will be forced to examine itself and, without a stable foundation of knowledge to stand on, is likely to cause enormous grief and uncertainty. The reason I have picked up this language and am writing this message to my followers is because I intend to lead this academic revolution.

The transformation will begin by releasing duplications of the scriptures followed by demands to see the authentic copy.

Slowly and with a hand of great precision, I will ignite the flame of doubt within my followers who will gradually gather kinetic energy that will overpower the corrupt rulers- who will thereafter be forced to relinquish their authority and further substantiate the claim that they are but mortal! This will be followed by the eventual reclamation of my throne, and this time with Tobias by my side.

Keep in mind that our constitutions and procedures hinder any writing of this type to be manufactured. Though my most treasured companion Prince Tobias, as he has taken the name after, has facilitated the deathly serious secret within the abode of our exile to reproduce the Word of God, as it has been called. We intend to create a cascade of emotional freedom and eliminate our modern world altogether from the Old Order.

My intentions to teach my followers this language will be difficult, but I am prepared for the undertaking. As a beginning, resurrecting this dead language will be the very tool that enhances our bonds and strikes dread into those who falsely believe in our old ways. I have written as much as I could within a decade while in exile for what I, for many a season, felt was my dishonor. That being having an intimate relationship with a member of my gender, which will now become my greatest strength. A public shame that will be overcome through the learning of both a language that predates our conception of history and the taking into questioning the tyrannical religion of the Second Civilization.

What this book revealed to me is, and likely was to our ancestors as much, inspiring. Because of it, our indoctrinated culture will be compelled to challenge the foundation of the belief system of today. The Bible serves as a pillar of doubt (as well as hope) of why we must not have a dogmatic approach to our societal quest to assent to a higher truth.

Through this revival of curiosity, we will break from the shackles of conformity, which has not only led us into the darkest of ages but also blinded us from the awareness that the rulers of this realm our use our education, that consists of ancient rituals and ceremonies, to control our behavior and with that strengthen their authority over us. Let this introduction be a warning that any civilization who advances to technological heights is at risk of destroying themselves. Let our disagreements be over how wonderful the imagination is or how brilliant our race can grow into and not about what gender a man loves or ancient recordings of pious superstition.

Made in the USA
Columbia, SC
22 July 2023